THE
SHADOW
GIRLS

BOOKS BY DAWN MERRIMAN

RYLAN FLYNN MYSTERY SERIES

The Spirit Girls

THE
SHADOW
GIRLS

DAWN MERRIMAN

SEC✶ND SKY

Published by Second Sky in 2023

An imprint of Storyfire Ltd.
Carmelite House
50 Victoria Embankment
London EC4Y 0DZ
United Kingdom

www.secondskybooks.com

ISBN: 978-1-83790-484-6
eBook ISBN: 978-1-83790-483-9

This book is dedicated to my husband, Kevin.
Thank you for all your help and your constant support.
I could not write these stories without you.

ONE

RYLAN FLYNN

The abandoned church surrounds me with silence and shadows. The quiet is so pure I can hear Mickey breathing behind me.

"I don't hear anything," she whispers from behind the camera.

The client that hired us said they often heard strange noises from the church on the edge of their property. Children laughing, moaning, footsteps, the usual disembodied sounds we run into investigating haunts.

"I don't hear anything either," I whisper back, disappointed. Although we get lots of calls about paranormal activity for our YouTube show, *Beyond the Dead*, it's rarely a ghost.

"Hello?" I try again, calling into the dark cavern of the sanctuary. The cross at the other end of the room glows, colorful in the pale moonlight, which pours through broken stained glass windows either side of the sanctuary. "If you are here, please show us."

We listen to the quiet, straining to hear anything from the other side. Mickey pans the camera around the room, then focuses back on me. "Do you want to try downstairs?" she whispers.

I nod. "We aren't getting any contact up here. Let's try the basement," I tell the camera.

Mickey films me walking down the dark stairs into an abyss of black, lit only by the light on her camera. Faintly, I hear laughter, the laughter of a child. A shiver runs across my shoulders.

I turn to Mickey. "Do you hear that?" My voice shakes with excitement.

Mickey looks around the camera, an expression of amazement on her face, then gives me a thumbs up, following me down the steps. "I'm not sure if the camera is picking it up," I say to my viewers, "but there is definitely a child laughing, or playing down here."

"I hear it," Mickey whispers.

I reach the bottom of the steps. A meeting room stretches before me, three doors hanging open to my right. The church used to have a daycare down here during the week.

The giggling is coming from the second door, a white slab with a handle. There's a three-inch gap between the door and the frame. Mickey follows as I make my way to the unassuming door.

Making sure Mickey is getting this on film, I reach for the handle. The laughter grows louder, a note of taunting in it.

I push the door into the room, expecting something to jump out at me.

The room is just as the daycare left it.

An overflowing toy box is in the far corner, the lid tightly closed.

A giggle comes from the toy box. I look to the camera and point to the box. My legs are heavy as I approach. "The laughter is coming from this box," I explain to the camera, not sure it is picking up the sounds.

The wooden toy box has peeling paint and stenciled letters on the lid. They are barely visible in the moonlight coming through the small basement window.

"Come find me," a small voice says from inside the box.

The sensation in my shoulders that tells me a spirit is near grows more intense. "The spirit said come find me," I tell the camera.

With a remarkably steady hand, I reach for the wooden lid. I slide a finger under, then throw it open.

The little boy bounds out, laughing and squealing. "You found me," he shouts.

I stumble backward, startled. He is on the move, running out the door into the large meeting room.

"I see him!" Mickey shouts. "I can see him!" She follows the boy with the camera, filming as he runs across the meeting room and up the stairs.

"You saw him?" I ask, dumfounded. Mickey never sees the ghosts.

"As plain as day," she says, breathlessly. "A boy about ten years old with dark hair? He was wearing a dark hoodie."

"That's him," I say.

I run into the meeting room in time to see the boy scurry up the stairs.

The boy is gone, but the shiver in my shoulders remains.

I return to Mickey in the daycare room. "He's gone."

"That was the son," a voice says, so quiet I can barely hear it.

I turn slowly toward the corner of the daycare room. "Mickey, over there," I say, pointing. Mickey's light moves to the corner, illuminating a woman in jeans and a loose-fitting floral shirt. "He comes here all the time," the figure says.

"I don't see anything," Mickey whispers.

"He messes with my things," the figure continues, walking to a desk at the far end of the room. She runs a hand lovingly over the items there: a stapler, a pile of papers, a notebook with red flowers on it. "He should stay at the house where he lives."

"Is that the Stinsons' son?" I ask.

"Yes. A naughty boy," the figure says.

I look to the camera. "It appears we've been tricked by the boy that lives on the property," I tell the viewers. "But this woman here is real."

Mickey shines the light on the desk where I'm pointing.

"Do you know why you are here?" I ask the spirit.

She studies my face. "No. I just come here to see the kids. But that Stinson boy is the only one I ever see." She runs a hand lovingly over the notebook on the desk. "He touches my things," she says again.

"How long have you been here?" I ask.

She looks past me at Mickey and the camera, then back to the notebook. "How long? I don't know."

"What's your name?"

"The kids call me Miss Melanie." She moves from behind the desk to a bookshelf in the corner. She runs a hand along the books. "Why can't I pick them up?" She looks at me with a pleading in her eyes. "I want to read to the children."

I hate this part of my job. It's hard telling them they are dead.

"You can't pick them up because you are only here in spirit," I tell Miss Melanie.

She turns so quickly I take an involuntary step back. "I am not a spirit. I am a teacher."

"I'm sorry, Miss Melanie, but you are deceased. Do you remember what happened?"

She looks down at her floral shirt, picks at the blue flowers. "Dead? How?"

"I don't know."

"Am I really dead?" she asks. "But who will look after the children?"

"This church has been abandoned for many years. All the children are grown now."

"Grown and gone?" she muses. "The wonderful and awful part of being a teacher. They always leave you."

"I'm so sorry."

Miss Melanie suddenly cocks her head, "Why are you here? How can you see me? Even the Stinson boy doesn't see me. I've told him to be more careful many times, but he never hears."

I dart my eyes to the camera and say, "She wants to know how I can see her." I turn back to Miss Melanie. "I'm Rylan Flynn, and this is my friend Mickey Ramirez. We came here to find you. The Stinson family had an idea that you were here and wanted me to help."

She looks confused. "Help how?"

"Help you cross to the other side."

She lifts her pale eyes to mine. "I won't leave the children."

"The children are gone, remember?"

She looks confused again, growing upset. "Stop saying that. They can't be gone and I can't be dead. You lie." She points to a corner. "Go stand in the corner for lying."

"I'm not lying," I say as gently as possible. "I'm here to help. I don't mean to upset you."

"That was the Stinson boy just now," she says again, seemingly forgetting the last few minutes. Ghosts have short memories.

"I saw him," I say. "He shouldn't come here and bother you, Miss Melanie."

She tips her head. "How do you know my name? Do I know you?"

"She's forgotten who I am," I tell the camera. "We should go."

I back away to leave her in peace. Mickey follows me out into the meeting room and up the steps to the sanctuary. Once away from Miss Melanie, I tell the camera all that was said.

Mickey finally turns it off and I breathe a sigh of relief that tonight's filming is over.

"That was intense," I say once we are back outside in the night. I lean against the brick railing on the stone steps. I feel hot, the night air cool on my cheeks.

"I thought I saw one," Mickey says. "Stupid kid. I thought he was a ghost and I actually saw him."

I put my arm around her shoulders. "Don't worry. It's not as much fun as you might think," I tell her.

"Would make my job easier. I could see what you see and hear what you hear instead of just filming your side of the conversation."

"Without you filming, there's no show."

"I suppose you're right," she concedes. We've had this conversation before.

"You know I'm right. I cannot do this show without you." I wait as she puts the camera safely in the backseat of the old tan Cadillac I inherited from my mother.

"Let's go tell the Stinsons what we found and make sure their son knows not to go into the church. Miss Melanie doesn't need the aggravation."

TWO

RYLAN FLYNN

After we talk to the Stinsons and walk across the driveway to the car, Mickey says, "You have an early morning tomorrow, don't you?"

"Ford asked me to give my official statement about what I saw of Kaitlyn's cousin the night she disappeared."

"So strange there hasn't been anything on Bess since you saw her leave the bar on Friday. How does someone disappear for days and no one see her?" Mickey climbs into the car as I take the driver's seat.

"Hard not to worry about the worst-case scenario," I say soberly.

Mickey looks out the window as we drive back into Ashby, Indiana. "Do you think she's been murdered?"

I've given it lots of thought since I found out I was the last one to see Bess Freeman before she disappeared. "I like to hope she's just off with that man she met at the bar having fun somewhere."

"Is that what Ford thinks?"

"The police always think that first. Usually, missing persons want to be missing. You know, a few days away from everyone."

"But Kaitlyn seemed pretty sure something bad happened," Mickey says.

"If you had to run a business with Kaitlyn every day, wouldn't you want to take some time off now and again? Let's not jump to conclusions. Hopefully Bess just went away for a few days and doesn't want to be bothered."

As Ford's ex-fiancé, Kaitlyn is not my favorite person. I try to console myself that he broke it off with her, but I was close to losing him forever.

Not that he's mine in any real way.

"I know you don't like Kaitlyn, but is that really what you think happened?"

I run a hand down my long brown hair nervously. "I want to believe that. She seemed happy with the guy I saw her with," I hedge.

"But you think something bad happened," she pushes.

"Honestly, I think a business partner would tell someone that they were leaving for a few days. Even if she thinks she's in love with this guy and they are on a romantic trip or something, I don't think she'd let the business suffer like that without a word," I say.

"I thought the same thing. I can't imagine you'd just take off without at least sending me a text, no matter who you met."

"Exactly."

"Which means she's in trouble."

We've stopped at a red light and I look fully at Mickey. "Yeah. I think she's in trouble."

"You have to get Ford to move on this."

"I'm sure he's already doing all he can."

Early the next morning, I sit at Ford's desk at the precinct giving my statement. "I really didn't get a good look at him," I protest.

"They were coming out the door and Bess fell into me. She had this long braid and it hit me in the face. She kind of laughed and then they left."

"Did she seem in distress or act strangely?"

I pick up a pen from his desk and twirl it between my fingers, thinking. "She seemed like she was having a good time. Relaxed and probably drinking. Honestly, I don't know what to tell you. You were inside the bar that night, too. Did you see her?"

Ford shakes his head. "I didn't notice her. The place was packed, though. Hard to see anything going on." He's disappointed. "So what did he look like? Anything will help."

I shut my eyes and think back to that moment. I get a fuzzy face in mind. "About thirty years old, maybe. Brown or sandy blond hair," I offer.

"Any facial hair?"

I squeeze my eyes tighter, try to focus on the memory. "A mustache? He might have had a mustache. He might not." I open my eyes. "Look, I don't really think I can be any help in this." I truly want to help, but I'm not giving him anything useful and it's frustrating me.

"You gave us something, that's a start. We'll get the video footage from The Lock Up and maybe see the guy on tape."

I relax a little and twirl his pen some more. "That would be good. I hate to think the whole case relies on my bare memory."

The phone on his desk rings. He listens a moment, his shoulders growing tight and his back straightening.

He darts his eyes to mine, says, "I'll be right there," and hangs up the phone.

"We'll have to finish this later." He pushes his chair back suddenly and stands.

I stand as well, confused at the sudden change. "What's wrong? Did something happen?"

He grabs the keys off his desk and shoves them in his pocket. "Some kids found some bones."

I raise my hand to my mouth, "Oh no. Is it Bess?"

He shakes his head. "Probably not. They are bones and she's only been missing a few days."

"Let me come with you. I might see something that will help."

"I can't let you do that." He's holding the door open, waiting for me to leave.

"You are in charge of the case, you can do what you need."

"Letting a civilian onto the scene is the last thing I need." Since our fright on the last case, we've been getting along famously. This hard-nosed man is the one I'm used to dealing with in the past. I'm not happy to see the return.

"But, I might help," I protest.

"It's not up to me. There's protocol. Everyone will be there." He's still holding the door, motioning for me to leave. I want to protest further, but it's futile. I walk past him into the hall. "You can't stop me from coming and standing outside the tape."

He sighs in resignation. "I suppose you're right. Just stay out of the way."

Once in the hall, I realize I'm still holding his pen. I slide it into my pocket.

The flurry of police activity and abundance of blue uniforms are a stark contrast to the lovely open lot on the outskirts of Ashby. The house that used to be on the lot is long gone, the only building an old barn that sags dangerously. A few stray leaves blow across the weedy yard and the early spring sun warms my skin. The police presence seems out of place.

The yellow tape blocks my entrance and I can't see very well, but the activity centers on a brushy area at the edge of the abandoned property. I can see Ford's blue polo shirt in the mix. Tyler is next to him as they squat and look at what the kids found.

I stretch onto the toes of my black Chuck Taylors to see what's going on.

"Do you know what they found?" a man standing next to me asks.

I don't look away from the scene. "I heard they found bones."

"Oh no," the man says. "That's not good."

"I know. I wonder who they belong to." I turn to face the man, but he has disappeared into the growing crowd of onlookers.

A tingle shivers down my back with the familiar feeling of a spirit nearby. I search the area around the rundown barn, around the bushes where they found the bones, around the overgrown lot. I'm hoping to see the owner of the bones.

If there's a spirit here, I can't see them.

Soon, the coroner's van pulls onto the scene and Dr. Marrero grumbles about the crowd as he ducks under the yellow tape. He spots me at the front of the onlookers.

"Can't stay away from trouble can you, Flynn?" he says.

I smile at the crotchety man. "I'm not bothering anything."

He waves a dismissive hand at me and joins Ford and Tyler.

Someone grabs my shoulder and squeezes hard. "It's not her, right?"

Kaitlyn Freeman is holding onto me, her fingers full of rings and her face full of terror.

"Ford said some kids found bones. Since they're bones and not a body, I don't think it could be Bess," I tell her.

Her shoulders visibly relax. "Oh, thank God. I heard that a body was found and I was just sure it was Bess."

"I'm sure it's not," I offer, gently shaking her hand off my shoulder, making her rings clack together. I have hated

Kaitlyn from afar for years, even before Ford asked her to marry him. It's surreal that she is talking to me at a crime scene now.

"But it's someone," she muses. "Some poor family's missing loved one."

She's right, and the solemnity of the situation strikes home. I know very well what it's like to lose a loved one to murder.

I suddenly want my mother.

My eyes sting and I wipe at them angrily. At least I still have Mom in some small way. This family won't have that luxury.

Kaitlyn and I stand in silence side by side as the police process the scene. We seem to be under a spell until they place the bones in a black body bag and roll them out on a gurney to the coroner's waiting van.

The crowd has grown, and the local news van is here. Officer Frazier is guarding the tape, looking less than pleased to be assigned that duty, shooting glares at the press.

When the body bag is brought out, people shift uncomfortably.

"Who is it?" someone shouts to Frazier.

He ignores the question, his face stoic.

"Do you know who they found?" another voice asks.

"You have to tell us something," a reporter says.

"They won't tell you anything," a woman says, so near my ear, I jump. I spin at the familiar voice. Lindy Parker looks smug that she startled me. "Not surprised to see you here, Rylan."

"Hey, Lindy," Kaitlyn says and gives her a quick hug. Of course they would know each other.

I wish Mickey was with me. I don't like being with my two least favorite people alone. I could use the backup of my best friend.

I feel someone watching and see Ford out of the corner of my eye. He seems very interested in our little group. I school my face into a placid expression, pretending to be fine with the two women.

"It's so sad," I offer to Lindy.

"You here to 'see' something?" Lindy asks with heavy sarcasm.

"I don't owe you an explanation," I say as sweetly as possible. "But maybe I can help."

"By being in the way," Lindy says.

Kaitlyn watches on with open interest. It's obvious she's on Lindy's side. The last hour of standing quietly together seems to be forgotten. Now that she has a friend with her, she's remembered she doesn't like me.

"I'm not in the way on this side." I point to the tape.

Ford ducks under the tape and I'm thankful for the intervention. He addresses Kaitlyn. "The bones are old," he says. "It's not Bess."

Kaitlyn falls into his arms in relief. I get the distinct feeling she's exaggerating her response and leaning on him to prove something to Lindy and me. Ford holds her stiffly, surprised.

When she wipes at her wet eyes, I feel bad for doubting her.

I shuffle my feet, uncomfortable watching Ford soothe her. Lindy is watching me closely.

"Thanks for letting us know it's not Bess," I say and back into the crowd.

"Rylan, wait," he calls. He releases Kaitlyn and steps closer. He lowers his voice so only I can hear. "Did you see any, you know?"

"Sadly, no. I'm sorry."

He steps away. "No reason to be sorry. It was a long shot."

Kaitlyn wriggles her arm into his like she has every right to touch him.

I don't want to look, so I turn on my sneaker-clad heel and push through the crowd.

Alone in my mom's Cadillac, I feel the tingle in my shoulders again. I search around, sure there's a ghost somewhere wanting to talk to me. All I see are the backs of heads. One man is looking in my direction, but focused on something behind me. I look over my shoulder, and the coroner's van is pulling away. When I look back, the man is watching the scene behind the tape again.

THREE

RYLAN FLYNN

As much as I want my mom right now, I can't bear to go home to my packed but empty house. I find myself driving out of Ashby and down the country road that leads to Aunt Val's. It is afternoon and the donut shop is closed, so I figure she'll be home. I could call, but I like surprising her.

Val and her black lab mix, George, sit on the front porch, enjoying the warm weather and sunshine. She raises a hand as I drive into the clearing.

A wave of love and acceptance flushes over me at the sight. Since Mom was murdered two years ago, Val has been like my second mother.

The steps creak as I climb to the front porch of her A-frame house. George wriggles his butt at my approach, shoves his wide black head under my hand for a rub. I happily oblige him.

"You done down at the precinct?" Val asks as I sit in my usual rocker with George at my feet.

"Been done for a while." I stare into the trees, framing my next words carefully. "Ford got called out on a new case. Some kids found bones in an abandoned lot on the edge of town."

Val sucks in a breath. "That's awful. It's not that missing woman is it?"

"Pretty sure the bones are older than Bess's remains would be."

Val shivers at my use of the word "remains." "Good for Kaitlyn, but bad for some other family."

"That's my exact thought." I continue to stare into the trees. "I wish there was something I could do to help. I was at the scene and I got the feeling there was a ghost nearby, but I didn't see anything."

"Were there a lot of people there?"

"Quite a few. Kaitlyn showed up thinking it was Bess. Oh, and Lindy Parker was there."

"Why would Lindy be there? Was she representing the DA or looking for info for her podcast?"

"I have no idea. Curious, I guess. She gave me some attitude, and I left."

"You don't have to be afraid of Lindy."

I bristle at that, pick at a spot of lint on my skinny jeans. "I'm not afraid of her. I just don't like being around her. She'll take anything I say and twist it, then blab about it on her show. I wish she'd find someone else to occupy her instead of trying to prove me a fake."

"You'd think she'd have learned you're the real deal by now. How long has she been hounding you?"

"For a few years. I swear she wasn't like that back in school. We had English together sophomore year and even did a project together. We got along fine."

"Wonder what changed her?"

I put my feet up on the porch rail and lean back in my chair. "I don't want to think about Lindy. She just likes to rattle me."

"So what are you going to do about the missing woman?"

"I've done all I can. I gave Ford my official statement, which wasn't much. I didn't even look at the guy that she was with. At least, not his face. I watched them walk away and that was that."

Val puts her feet up next to mine. "That's that, huh?" she says with heavy disbelief.

"What else can I do?"

Out of the corner of my eye, I can see Val's shrug. "Do what you do."

I take my feet down. "How can that help in this situation? Hopefully, Bess is still alive so she isn't a ghost. Besides that, I don't know what I bring to the table."

Val closes her eyes, seems completely at ease. "You'll figure it out."

I lean forward. "You're impossible. I'm not part of the investigation into Bess or into the bones that were found this morning."

Val smiles, her eyes closed. "Something tells me that will change."

"Like I said, you're impossible." I look back into the trees surrounding her small house, watch the sun dance on the leaves.

Val makes a sound of contentment. "It is so nice to be back home. I missed this."

The reference to Val's recent time in custody taints the serene scene. "I'm so sorry that happened to you."

Val doesn't open her eyes. "It sucked, I won't lie. But I'm home now."

George raises his head from his paws and pushes his nose against my leg. I rub him behind the ears. "You're home now."

"Home," she sighs.

My phone chimes its text tone.

"I wonder who that could be," Val says knowingly, a smile twitching at her lips.

I check the screen, surprised to see Ford's name. "It's Ford. 'Can you come to the precinct tomorrow to go over the footage from The Lock Up?'"

"Told you." Val opens her eyes and sits forward.

"This doesn't mean I'm involved."

She puts a hand on my knee. "Rylan, my dear, you're involved whether you know it or not."

"What does that mean?"

"That boy can't stay away from you any better than you can stay away from him."

My face suddenly burns. "I don't know what you're talking about. Besides, he's helping Kaitlyn."

"Keep telling yourself that." She gives a little laugh and stands. "Now, have you eaten?"

"You sound like Mom." I instantly regret the words.

Val cocks her head in curiosity and looks suddenly sad. She opens her mouth to say something, but shuts it again without a word. Silence hangs over the porch. "I was going to make coney dogs. Do you want some?" she finally asks, changing the subject from Mom.

I bounce out of my chair. "Coneys are my favorite," I say.

"That's why I'm making them," she says, following me inside.

The kitchen glows like home, nothing like my crowded, hoarded house. As Val heats up the hot dogs, I stare out the window into the woods. At the edge of the clearing, a shadow shifts. I look closer, but can't see anything. I press my face close to the window, my nose touching the cool glass.

"You okay?" Val asks.

I turn away from the window. "Déjà vu, I think."

Val looks thoughtful, but changes the subject. "How many dogs you want?"

I take a seat at the kitchen bar and push thoughts of bones and ghosts and moving shadows out of my mind.

FOUR

FORD PIERCE

Silly that I was hoping Rylan would see something here at the crime scene. I tell myself that I let her come along because I need to look at all the angles. Really, I know if she could see the dead victim, talk to them, it would make my job a lot easier. I watch Rylan leave, then look down to see Kaitlyn's arm still linked with mine.

"Strange girl," Kaitlyn says after Rylan is gone. I pointedly remove my arm from her grip.

"She's not that strange."

"She sees ghosts for a living," Kaitlyn says.

"She 'claims' to see ghosts," Lindy Parker adds. "That's not the same as actually seeing them."

I glare at Lindy. When I was dating Kaitlyn, Lindy was often part of our friend group. I'd see her at parties and get-togethers. I never understood why Kaitlyn was friends with her, though. She's always so snarky.

I don't like how she's made her hobby trying to prove Rylan is a fake in her podcast. She should stick to her work at the DA's office.

I turn away from both women and duck back under the yellow tape, glad they can't follow me.

My partner, Tyler Spencer, is talking to one of the crime scene techs who is taking pictures of the brushy area where the bones were found. The way she's looking at him makes me wonder if they are talking about the scene or something more personal.

The tech's cheeks turn a darker shade of pink and she looks down. She's definitely interested. For his part, Tyler seems oblivious. Or maybe I just can't see it.

I interrupt the conversation. "Anything new?" I ask the tech, whose name escapes me.

She looks contrite. "Nothing in the last few minutes," she says. "They are searching the barn now."

The sagging barn is the only building left on the empty lot. I'm surprised that whoever hid the body in a shallow grave didn't put it in the barn. Maybe bury it under the dirt in one of the stalls.

I shudder when I realize the barn may hold more bodies.

Tyler follows my quick footsteps through the tall weeds to the open doors. Techs in Tyvek suits mill around inside, the afternoon sun falling on them through the many cracks in the walls. Dust kicked up from their movements dances in the shafts of light. It's almost pretty.

The ceiling looks like it might fall in at any moment. A bird, startled by all the movement, suddenly flies around the rafters, then darts toward my head.

I duck, flinching. "Stupid bird," I say, nervously.

Tyler smiles at my reaction. "It was just a sparrow."

"It nearly hit me in the head." I have only taken a step or two into the building but I don't want to go any further.

"Anything?" Tyler asks the head tech.

The tech shakes his head. "Just rotting straw and lots of raccoon droppings."

"Is that what smells so bad?" Tyler asks.

The tech smiles. "Yeah. It's not decomp if that's what you mean. Just an old barn."

I take a quick glance around the decrepit building, empty except for piles of molding hay up in the loft and bales of black straw in one corner. "Looks like it's been abandoned for a long time," I say.

"I don't think we'll find anything in here," the head tech says.

We thank him and step back into the sunlight. I'm thankful to be out of the creepy barn.

"Well, I think we've done all we can here today," I say to Tyler. "Let's go back to the precinct and go over missing-persons reports to see if we can come up with a possible for the bones."

"How far back do you think we should look?"

"So hard to tell. Maybe Marrero will be able to determine more."

"Would have been too much to wish for scraps of clothes or an ID with the bones," Tyler muses as we climb into our car.

"Why make it easy?" I say, starting the car.

He hesitates and then says, "I saw Rylan Flynn was here. She didn't happen to see anything, did she?"

The note of hopefulness in his voice would be almost comical if I hadn't had the same hope earlier. "She says she didn't."

"Like you said, why make it easy," he says, buckling his seat-belt. "Any new leads from the statement she gave you this morning."

"The guy may or may not have had a mustache," I say with an edge of sarcasm.

"That's helpful. When's the video footage from The Lock Up coming in?"

"I'd hoped we'd see it this morning. The owner is not happy

to have his bar involved. He's dragging his feet on getting the footage to us."

"Wonder what he's hiding?"

I look at Tyler, not surprised he had the same thought I did. "I explained that we only were interested in the parts involving Bess and, if we saw anything else, it wasn't really our concern."

"Still, we don't have the videos yet."

"Sure makes me curious."

───────

Tyler and I spend the rest of the afternoon pouring over missing-persons reports going back years. Ashby is not a huge town and most missing persons show up after a few days. There's not much to go on, so we search nearby towns too.

There's a few from a decade ago that might match. A woman that was reported by her brother, but her husband said she ran off with another man. That one could fit. Marrero said the bones were female, but refused to give any other information.

The case of a young boy that went for a bike ride and never returned is still open from two decades ago. The bones were of an adult woman, so they don't belong to the boy.

"I think this might be it," Tyler says, showing me his computer screen. "Disappeared from a bar out on Highway 7."

"When was this?" I roll my chair around our facing desks to see his screen.

"Three years ago. Depending on what Marrero says, it could fit the timeframe. The body could have skeletonized in that time, since the grave was shallow."

I read over the details of the case. "She was reported by her sister," I read. "They had drinks then the sister left her at the bar."

"Witnesses said she left with a man, and she was never seen again."

I look closer at the screen. "What was her name?"

"Melanie Shaw. Age twenty-seven."

"Melanie Shaw? Why does that sound familiar?" I roll back around the desks.

"Wasn't in our jurisdiction, but I remember the case. There was a bit of media coverage, then it died down. I honestly figured she came home, but it shows as an open case."

"Would help if we knew more about the bones." I check my phone, as if it will suddenly ring with a call from the coroner.

"You know he won't tell us anything until he's completely done."

"How long does it take to examine bones?" I huff.

"As long as it takes." Tyler turns back to his computer. "I'm going to keep looking."

A uniformed officer knocks on our open door. "A package just came for you two," he says, handing me a manila envelope.

I thank the officer and tear open the package. Inside are two thumb drives and a handwritten note from the owner of The Lock Up.

Hope you find what you're looking for.

Tyler sits up straight, excited to finally have the footage from Bess's disappearance. "Movie time," he says, plugging the first of the thumb drives into his computer.

The screen flickers a few times and then the footage from the bar area plays. We watch for a long time on fast forward as patrons come in and out of the frame. The bar is crowded and it's hard to make out faces, but it's a long time until Bess makes an appearance.

She's recognizable from her long braid as she orders a drink, taking a seat at the bar. She sips it alone, her head bobbing in time to the music of the band.

We watch for a long time; she orders another drink.

"I don't see anyone," I say after a long time of watching. Bess seems lonely, sad even. Seeing her drinking alone on what might be the last night of her life breaks my heart.

"Wait," Tyler says as a new man enters the frame. "Is that the guy?"

The man has his back to the camera as he leans close to Bess, talking near her ear. She smiles and throws back her head, laughing at whatever he said. He orders her a drink, and takes a seat next to her, all the while keeping his face away from the camera.

"Do you think he's purposely avoiding the camera?" I ask.

"Looks like it. He's definitely careful."

We watch as the two get to know each other, sliding closer as the night wears on. After an hour or so, they suddenly stand and cross out of frame.

"Are they leaving already?" Tyler asks.

I check the time stamp. "No. I didn't get there until later and Rylan came after me. They must be moving to a table."

"Let's check the other thumb drive."

As suspected, the other drive holds the video from a different camera, one that captures the entire room. We fast forward to the time Bess and the man arrive at a table. In the very corner of the frame, we watch them take a small table in the back of the bar. They are so far away it's hard to make out any details. Still, the man keeps his face from the camera.

"Think he knows where they are or he just got lucky?" Tyler asks.

"I think he did his homework and knows where all the cameras are. That makes this premeditated for sure. I wonder if he chose Bess at random or he targeted her."

"Maybe he's been watching for the right woman. Someone alone and vulnerable."

We watch the tiny, grainy figures on the screen. At one point, Bess leaves the table and goes to the restroom. Other than that, the couple stays at the table together.

Finally, they head to the front door and cross out of frame.

"Well, that wasn't very helpful," Tyler says, stopping the video.

"Not really."

"Maybe Rylan can see something that we missed. She could at least confirm that the guy on the video is the same one she saw leaving with Bess."

"Or she picked up a new man on the way out with this one?" I say sarcastically.

Tyler shrugs. "To be thorough, we should have her confirm."

He's right and I know it. I send her a quick text. "There. She's coming tomorrow."

FIVE

RYLAN FLYNN

I pull on my black leather ankle boots and climb over the piles of clothes, blankets, and stuffed animals that fill my room. Boxes line the walls like protective bricks, and the soft things in the center create a cocoon. I love my room. Only here do I feel truly safe.

I open the door onto the similarly filled hall, careful to hug the wall as I pass the room Keaton used as a boy. Nothing beats on Keaton's door this morning.

Mom's door is open as always. I peak inside and she's sitting at her dressing table trying to rearrange the many items she left there the night she was murdered. Her hand goes through the perfume bottles. She scrunches her lips in concentration and a tube of lipstick moves at her touch. She smiles in victory. "I did it," she whispers.

When she notices me at the door, watching, she turns quickly and runs her hands down her blood-stained nightgown in a nervous gesture.

"I didn't know you were there," she says, jumping from the chair guiltily.

"What are you doing?" I'm curious what she thinks is going

on. In all the time I've known her as this spirit, in the years since her murder, she's never let on that she realizes she's a ghost.

"It's the strangest thing, I can't move the perfumes, but if I try really hard, I can move the lipstick." She sounds genuinely confused. I want to tell her the truth. I used to tell her about how I found her shot in the head in this very room, in the bed behind her. I used to explain what I know of the world beyond.

Then she'd forget and it was too painful to tell her again. Eventually, I quit telling her.

"That's strange," I hedge. "Keep trying and maybe it will get easier." I do know that spirits can sometimes move things on this side if they try hard enough.

Mom looks at my leather jacket and boots. "You look pretty. Where are you going?"

I chose this pair of black skinny jeans and my leather jacket because I know they look good, but I don't want it to be too obvious that I tried with my outfit.

"I'm going to look at some video with Ford."

"Ooh, like a date?" she coos.

"No. Nothing like a date."

How I wish.

"Oh." She looks at the ground confused. "Okay, have fun." She takes the brush from the bed, looks at it curiously, then runs it through her hair. When I found her body, she had the brush in her hand, so it is with her in death. No wonder she can't figure out why she can move the brush but not other things.

She turns her back to me and I look away from the shattered hole in her head. In all this time with her ghost living in this house, I have not gotten used to the hole.

I will never get used to it.

I stop at Aunt Val's donut shop and pick up two coffees on my way to the precinct. When I see Tyler in the office with Ford, I realize I should have gotten three. I've already sipped half of mine or I would offer it to Tyler.

"Uh, I got you coffee," I say to Ford, handing him a cup with the green The Hole logo on the side. "Sorry, I didn't get you one," I say to Tyler. "I didn't know you'd be here."

He smiles politely from his chair. "No worries." He smothers a chuckle and I get the feeling I'm the butt of a joke I don't understand.

I look to Ford for support, a question in my eyes. "Don't mind him. He's just in a weird mood this morning." He shoots Tyler a look to shut him up. "Don't you have other work you should be doing?"

Tyler sobers and says, "Sorry. Yes, I do." He grabs a folder from his desk and heads out the door. "You two have fun," he says over his shoulder.

"Is he okay?" I ask, embarrassed, but not entirely sure why.

"He's just messing with us. He was teasing me about this being a movie date earlier. He thinks he's funny."

It's so close to what Mom said, it makes my cheeks burn. "So, the video?" I change the subject.

"Right. I've got it cued up here on my computer. I just need to make sure this is the same man you saw Bess leave with."

He pulls Tyler's chair around the desks and offers it to me. We sit and watch the grainy video together. I look at Bess drinking her beer alone, my heart hurting, wondering where she could be now. A man joins her and strikes up a conversation. Even though the video is not good, it's obvious she is enjoying the attention.

"I can't see his face," I say. "Like I said before, I never got a good look at him, but that could be the same man."

"Look closer. Be sure."

I lean closer to the monitor and study the images. "He has a mustache. I'm pretty sure the man I saw did, too."

"Does he look familiar? Have you seen him anywhere else? Ashby is a small town, you might know him."

I lean in again. "No." I shake my head. "I think I'd remember that mustache. It's like a huge caterpillar."

Ford sighs. "That's what I thought. It's almost too full. It's like the only thing we can see of his face."

"Meaning?"

"We think it's a fake."

I look at the screen again, at the sliver of profile I can see. "Yeah, you might be right. I wonder if Bess noticed it was fake."

"She can't have. Not if she left with him."

"If she was as lonely as she seems in the early part of this video, she might not have cared."

"I noticed that, too. The guy must have, also. That's probably why he picked her. We ran the video back to earlier, but can't find him anywhere. He knew where the cameras were and how to avoid them. Only when he joins her at the bar do we get any view of him."

I sit back in my chair. "So now what?"

"I think we're done for now." He sits back in his chair, too.

I run the charms on my bracelet through my fingers one at a time, a nervous habit. "What about the bones from yesterday? Did you find out whose they are?"

He looks at me, considering how much to share. "Marrero says they belong to a woman aged between twenty and thirty-five. Beyond that, we don't know."

I can tell he's not giving me all the details. "But you have an idea who it might be."

He rubs his face in thought, then sits forward so fast it startles me. "It will be public information soon, anyway," he grumbles, grabbing a blue folder. "The bones match a missing-persons report from a few years ago." He flips the folder open. "Melanie Shaw."

"Another Melanie. Hmm."

"What do you mean another?"

"Mickey and I just filmed a show. The ghost said her name was Melanie. Where did this woman disappear from?"

"From a bar out on Highway 7. Just over the county line, so not our jurisdiction."

"That doesn't really match where we were last night. We were in the opposite side of town from that. Out in the country on Knopp Road."

"The abandoned church at the corner of that old farm?"

I look at him with surprise. "You know the place?"

"I've been by it lots of times. So that church is haunted? It looks like it would be."

"There's at least one spirit there. She was a teacher in the daycare there."

"But that church has been falling down for years and Melanie Shaw disappeared only three years ago."

I twist a strand of my hair, thinking. "Yeah, that doesn't line up. Must be a coincidence." I feel deflated. I thought I was onto something.

"We're not even sure it is Melanie Shaw we found. Marrero is running dental records but that will take time." Ford stands. "I appreciate you coming down to look at the video."

"Sorry I couldn't be more help."

"Too bad he knew where the cameras were and didn't look at them. That would at least have given us somewhere to start. All we have is a middle-aged man with short brown hair who might have a mustache."

"Did the owner or the bartender recognize him?"

"They've all been questioned. The bartender said she remembers seeing the two of them, but he wouldn't look directly at her. The bar was packed that night. She's in the same position you are. Saw him, but didn't really see him."

"Seems like he knew what he was doing. Do you think this is the first time he's taken a woman home and she disappeared?"

"We've checked the files, but nothing is standing out. A few other missing women that we are looking into, but nothing that matches this MO."

I stand in the doorway, hesitant to leave. "Do you have any other leads on Bess? Anything at all?"

Ford's shoulders sag. "Nothing. Kaitlyn has told us everything she can think of. We've talked to all the employees at their clothing company and to all Bess's friends and family. No one has any idea where she might be. Kaitlyn is out of her mind with worry."

"I bet." I don't want to feel sorry for Kaitlyn. I don't want to think of her at all.

"Thanks again," he says. He picks up the cup of coffee I brought. "And thanks for the coffee."

I know I should leave, but my feet don't seem to agree. "Uh, right, yeah," I stammer.

A smile twitches at the corners of his mouth. "You okay?"

"Yes. Look, you'll keep me in the loop on this case, right? I might be able to help. Maybe we can go out to talk to the Melanie I met at the church. It's a long shot, but she could be the same Melanie."

Ford takes a long time to answer. "You want me to interview a ghost?"

I toe the dirty linoleum with my leather boot, feeling foolish. "I mean, if you think it might help."

He smiles suddenly. "Okay, but don't tell Tyler."

SIX

RYLAN FLYNN

The abandoned church looks different in the daylight. What was a dark, hulking mass is just a dilapidated brick building now. It's sad and sagging. I'm surprised the tall bell tower that reaches into the blue, cloudless sky is still standing.

"I called and asked the Stinsons if we could visit again," I tell Ford as he climbs out of his car in the small parking area. The gravel lot is full of so many weeds the stones are barely visible. I wonder if the Stinsons have to mow it.

Ford studies the building. "You sure it's safe to go inside?"

"Mickey and I went." I start up the stone steps.

He shakes his head. "And I thought I had a dangerous job. You faced a falling-down building and a ghost in the dark."

"Ghosts aren't really dangerous. They just want to be heard. That's why they make so much noise." It's an inside joke, one that Mickey and I share. Ford gives me a strained smile.

"Do you think your Miss Melanie will talk to us in the middle of the day like this?"

"Well, usually we do these visits at night, but that's really more because it makes it dramatic for the camera." I think of

Mom and how she appears at all times of the day. "Spirits kind of do what they want."

He follows me to the front steps and takes a deep breath. "Ready?"

I see the deep breath and tension in his face. "Are you scared?" I tease.

"No," he replies too quickly.

"She won't hurt you."

"I've never talked to a ghost, is all."

"You'll be fine, tough guy." I pat him on the shoulder as I walk past him and up the stairs.

He looks up at the brick bell tower. "Hope that thing doesn't collapse."

"Stop worrying."

The inside of the church is as silent as last time. The birds' chirping from the trees barely penetrates the walls. A kind of reverence hangs in the air. The pews have been removed and the small sanctuary is full of leaves, blown in through the broken windows.

"Wow, this place is rough," Ford whispers.

I stand perfectly still, listening, feeling. A tiny shock travels up my back.

"She's here," I whisper.

Ford turns pale. "You sure?"

I give him a reassuring smile. "Only one way to find out." I lead him to the stairs that go to the basement and the daycare room, the place we saw Miss Melanie last time.

A smell of rot fills our noses as we enter the meeting room at the bottom of the steps.

"That's awful," Ford says, putting his hand to his nose. "What is it?"

"Old building. Maybe a dead rat or something. Abandoned places often smell like this," I whisper. "The room we saw her in is right here."

I wait outside the half-open door. Ford pushes close behind me, so close I can hear him breathing. The tiny basement windows barely illuminate the meeting room. Through the next door, inside the daycare room, it is dark.

I touch the door and push it open a few more inches. "Miss Melanie?" I lean into the opening.

A familiar shiver shakes my body. I look at the desk far to the right. She stands behind it.

"I see her," I tell Ford. A sharp intake of breath is his response.

"I don't." He sounds disappointed.

"Miss Melanie, it's Rylan. We met before."

Melanie shifts her head to look at me. "Before?"

I step into the dim room, one eye on the colorful toy box, half-expecting the Stinson boy to burst out again. "My friend, Mickey, and I came to see you," I explain. "We talked."

Melanie tips her head, then notices Ford behind me. She smiles brightly at him. "And who's this?"

"She sees you." I say over my shoulder. "Introduce yourself."

"I'm Detective Ford Pierce. Nice to meet you, Miss Melanie." He looks in the direction I'm looking.

"I don't get many visitors. Especially not nice-looking strangers," she says, her eyes on the floor.

I stifle a laugh. "She thinks you're nice looking."

"Thank you," he says to the space behind the desk. "Can we ask you a few questions?"

Melanie smiles brightly. "Anything for you."

"She says yes."

Ford hesitates, looking at me for guidance. "Does she know why she's here?" he asks in a very low voice.

"I doubt it." I look to Melanie. "Do you know how long you have been here?"

Melanie looks thoughtful. "The kids don't come. Where are the kids?"

"I'm sorry they don't come," I say. "How long has it been since you've seen them?"

She looks thoughtful. "I don't know," she says vaguely. "I seem to lose track of time so easily these days."

"She's been losing track to time," I repeat for Ford's benefit.

"How long have you been losing track of time?" Ford asks.

Melanie gives him a tight smile. "That's a strange question. If I could keep track of time, I could answer you."

I tell Ford what she said and he concedes the point.

I try a different tactic. "What's the last thing you remember before the kids stopped coming."

"That's personal," she says too quickly.

"It's okay," I soothe. "You can tell us."

She looks uncomfortable, keeps her eyes on the toy-strewn floor. "I was at a bar."

"She was at a bar," I tell Ford. Excitement fills me.

"Was that the Juke Joint on Highway 7?" Ford asks.

Melanie lifts her eyes from the floor. "How did you know?"

"It was," I say, my voice beginning to shake. "Melanie, is your last name Shaw?"

Her eyes grow wide. "How do you know all this? I don't know you. We just met."

"It's her," I tell Ford.

"How did you die? Did the guy you met kill you?" Ford asks, his own voice full of excitement.

Melanie's eyes grow round and she takes a step back. "I'm not dead!" she shouts. "How dare you."

"Please, Melanie. You have to help us," I say. "She's upset," I say to Ford.

"I want you to go. You are telling lies. We don't allow liars here."

"Miss Melanie, please. What is the last thing you remember from before?" I push.

"Go away! I'm calling for help and he will make you leave. Reed! Reed, make them go away."

She cowers behind the desk, her face in her hands. I'm ashamed of us for upsetting her.

"She's calling for help. We should go. She's really upset."

I back away from the crying spirit and Ford follows me out the door and up the steps to the main sanctuary. "Is she really Melanie Shaw?"

"She all but said she was, before she got upset," I say as we exit the crumbling building.

"The timeline doesn't work out well, though. Melanie Shaw could not have worked here at this daycare," Ford says as we go down the front steps.

"Yeah, I guess you're right. That's strange."

"Still, we just talked to the owner of the bones we found," he says in disbelief. "That's amazing." He raises his eyes to meet mine. "You are amazing."

Something inside me melts under his deep blue gaze. My chest feels tight. "Thank you," I say, breathless.

He leans an inch or two toward me, the tension between us thick.

Then his phone rings.

Whatever spell we were under shatters at the sound.

"It's Kaitlyn. I have to take this."

My heart sinks as he says hello. "Okay, I'll come now," he tells her. He puts his hand over the phone and says to me, "We done here?"

"Yeah, we're done," I say with finality.

SEVEN

FORD PIERCE

I'm a little shaken by the encounter with Miss Melanie's ghost. Part of me wants to think Rylan faked the whole thing. I didn't actually see Melanie, or hear her. Only Rylan did. I had hoped to see her.

But I believe Rylan.

As I drive to Kaitlyn's apartment, I shift my mind from Melanie's case to Bess's. Kaitlyn wants an update and I don't have anything new to tell her. She also said that she wants to show me something that might help the case.

I know the way to the apartment well. Until a few months ago, I lived here with her. Now I have my own apartment across town, close to the precinct. I haven't been in this complex since the day I left and it feels a bit odd to be here now.

My usual parking spot is empty and I take it with an eerie sense of déjà vu. I walk up the landscaped path, admiring the yellow spring flowers. This complex is nicer than where I live now.

But I'm free.

Outside Kaitlyn's door, I pause. Knocking seems strange, but I raise my hand and do it anyway.

The door opens so quickly, I get the feeling she was waiting for me behind it.

"You came," she says softly.

"I told you I would." I stand outside on the landing, taking a deep breath. I've not been alone with Kaitlyn like this since I walked out the same door.

She steps back. "Come in."

I'd rather talk to her out here in the open, but that would be rude. I step inside.

The apartment is mostly the same. Same brown, overstuffed couch, same glass coffee table. The recliner that used to sit in the corner went with me. There's a tall potted plant in that spot now.

"The place looks good," I say. I fight the urge to shove my hands in my pockets. I don't want her to know this visit is rattling me.

"Please, sit." She motions to the couch.

I decline the offer. "I don't have any new information on Bess, but we are doing all we can."

She stares at me hard. "Nothing? She's been missing five days. You have to find her."

"Like I said, we're doing all that we can."

"Did you talk to that ghost girl? She said she saw the man that was with her."

For a moment, I think she's talking about Melanie and wonder how she knew what we just did. But she's talking about Rylan. I bristle at the slight. "Rylan has been helping as much as she can. She didn't get a good look at the man. She even went over the video from the bar and confirmed that the man with Bess was the same man she left with. Unfortunately, the video camera never got a clear shot of his face."

She wraps her arms across her chest. "So you don't know who she was with?"

I shake my head.

Kaitlyn's expression is a mixture of fear and sadness. It then turns hopeful. "Maybe this will help." She turns to the bar between the living area and the kitchen, and the laptop sitting there. "I broke into her computer," she says proudly.

"Broke in?"

"Well, I spent some time guessing the password. It wasn't really that hard. She only has a few passwords and uses them for everything."

I look at the Gmail account open on the screen. "What did you find?"

"Mostly work stuff. She did all the buying at the company and most of the emails are about clothing orders for the store."

"Okay," I say cautiously. "How does that help find her?"

"I don't know. Isn't that your job? I see it all the time on TV where they go through the computer and find evidence."

"Did you find anything that might be evidence?"

She squints at the screen. "I haven't read everything yet. I just got in this morning. I'm hoping your expert can find something." She slides the computer to me. "Here, take it. See what you can do." She shuts the computer with a snap.

"I'll take it," I say gently. "But don't get your hopes up."

"My hopes are about as low as they can get," she sniffles.

"We really are doing all we can." She sniffs in disbelief. "We really are."

"Don't let this get pushed to the back burner now that you found those bones yesterday. It's too late for the bones, but Bess is still out there."

I pick up the computer and walk to the door. "I'm sure she is."

I wish I believed my own words.

Back at the precinct, I turn the computer over to the tech department, but I don't have much hope that they will find anything useful. It looked very much like she just met the man that she left with. I seriously doubt they had been exchanging emails.

Tyler is in our office, typing furiously. At least for him. He's mostly a hunt-and-peck typist and he's stabbing the keyboard now.

I watch from the doorway for a moment. "What's up?"

He lifts his head, startled. "What do you mean?"

"You're practically punching that keyboard." I take my seat at the desk facing his.

He shoves the keyboard away. "This paperwork is backing up. I have better things to do than typing."

"There's always paperwork. You don't normally torture the keyboard over it."

He shoves back in his chair and stares at me. He opens his mouth like he's going to say something, then closes it again. He picks up a pen and chews on the end of it.

"Don't torture the pen, too," I tease.

He throws the pen at my head and I duck away with a laugh.

"Mind your own business." He sits forward. "Where've you been all morning?"

I had debated with myself during the drive here on what to tell Tyler about my excursion with Rylan. I decided on the truth.

"I went with Rylan to that old church out on Knopp Road."

He leans onto his elbows. "Why would you do that?"

I run a hand over my short hair, stalling. "Well."

"You might as well spill it. I can see you're dying to tell me."

"We went to talk to the ghost of Melanie Shaw."

"The ghost of Melanie Shaw? The woman Marrero is doing a dental record check on this very moment?"

"The same Melanie Shaw." I nod smugly. "Rylan met her last night while filming for her show. She didn't know it was the same Melanie, but we went to confirm. It is."

He sits up straighter. "You talked to the ghost?"

"Well, I talked, but I didn't see her and I couldn't hear her. Rylan did, though."

He lets out a long breath. "That's so cool. So she told you who killed her? This is huge."

I sink back in my chair. "I wish. She kind of freaked out when we told her she was dead. She made us leave."

"She didn't know she was dead?"

"Guess not. Rylan said they often don't know what's happened to them."

"So she didn't say Bob so and so killed me?" he muses. "Guess it can't be that easy."

"But we talked to her. From the other side."

Silence fills the office for a few moments as that fact sinks in.

"This is crazy," Tyler finally says. "You sure Rylan didn't fake it?"

"You've seen her show. You know she's the real deal."

Another few moments of quiet.

"Wow," he says.

"I know."

"Next time"—he leans forward—"take me with you."

I'd expected derision, but he's smiling from ear to ear.

EIGHT

RYLAN FLYNN

After the late night talking to Miss Melanie and then visiting her again today, I'm tired. Seeing the beyond takes a toll on my mental and emotional energy.

And seeing Ford leave me to go to Kaitlyn didn't help either.

A nap sounds really good, but I'm late for Mickey's.

"Blue Bayou" by Linda Ronstadt plays on the car radio. Her sad crooning matches my mood as I drive through Mickey's neighborhood.

I am empty.

I am alone.

I feel useless. I should be out finding Bess. I should be trying to find out who killed Miss Melanie.

A quick check of the time shows I'm later than I thought.

I should have been here ten minutes ago.

I knock on Mickey's front door, then let myself in. "Sorry I'm late," I shout down the hall. A lovely smell of garlic and onion fills the house.

Mickey's husband, Marco, pokes his head around the wall to the kitchen. "She's in the office. You staying for dinner?"

"If it tastes as good as it smells, how could I say no?" I hurry down the hall to Mickey's office studio. The door is closed. She usually leaves it open for me. I knock, but she doesn't answer. I turn the knob and let myself in.

Mickey has on headphones and is leaning toward the computer, deep in editing.

I touch her on the shoulder and she jumps. Her jump makes me jump.

"Holy flip, you scared me." I laugh as she pulls off her headphones.

"You scared me first."

"Guess I'm a little jumpy." I sink into my usual chair and sigh. "I'm in a strange mood."

Mickey eyes me intently. "Something happen? Did they find Bess?"

"Not yet. I wish. I'm just a little off because I went with Ford to see Miss Melanie today."

"You went back to the church with Ford? Why?"

"Those bones that were found yesterday might have belonged to her." I push my hair out of my face. "Turns out they are hers, at least we think so."

Mickey just looks at me for a beat. "She was murdered?"

"Looks like it."

"How?"

"I don't know. I don't think the coroner is done, at least Ford didn't say anything. I didn't see anything obvious on her. No gunshots or injuries that I could tell. But it's dark in the daycare room and I didn't get a good look."

"Did you ask her?"

"We both know they don't always know how they died. Melanie freaked out when we even mentioned it."

"So we don't have a show again." Mickey's always the practical one. "We can't use the footage of a murder victim, not when the case is open."

"We could use last week's."

"That's a little fresh, too."

I lean back in my chair. "What do you want to do?"

She clicks on her computer and pulls up the *Beyond the Dead* email account. "Guess we'll have to follow up on some of these emails." She scans the list of requests for us to investigate possible hauntings.

I pull my chair close and read along with her. "This one might work. It's right here in Ashby. Cold spots and a sense of a presence."

"That's not much to go on."

"We've done shows with less."

Mickey reads through the email again. "Isn't that the address of your dad's church?"

I check. "Huh! No, but it's the same street."

"Give them a call. See if we can do it tonight. We need something."

Turns out the house in question is right next door to Dad's church. It's a Victorian mansion I've long admired. The church's small cemetery is between the two historic buildings. The green roofs contrast beautifully with the stark white paint. I often imagined sipping tea on one of the porches, or reading a book in one of the turrets.

It is too beautiful to be a traditional haunted house, but it's close.

The porch doesn't even squeak when we cross it, everything is so well cared for.

"This place is amazing," Mickey whispers as I push the ornate door bell.

"I know. I can't believe we are getting to go inside."

"You getting anything?" Mickey asks.

I do a mental check of my body. "I always get the tingles when I am this close to that cemetery. There's definitely something near, but I don't know if it's from the house."

The heavy wooden door suddenly opens and a young couple greets us. "You must be the ghost hunters," the husband says sarcastically. Not a good start.

"I'm Rylan and this is Mickey," I say, reaching to shake his hand. He glances at my hand but doesn't take it. He looks decidedly nervous. I drop my hand back to my side awkwardly.

"I'm Candy Carrillo and this is Antonio," the woman says, taking my hanging hand and stepping back to lead us inside. She is much more inviting than her husband. "I am so glad you could come. We've been at our wit's end."

We step into the grand house, and I have to force myself to keep my mouth from dropping open at all the carved wood and the massive fireplace with marble carvings on either side. Everywhere I look there is something beautifully carved. It is easily the most stunning old house we've ever investigated. Candy notices our reactions. "It's a bit overwhelming, isn't it?" she asks.

"It is beyond lovely," Mickey says. "Did you do the restoration yourselves?"

Antonio makes a sound of derision. "If we had done it, I'd have made it modern. All this fancy woodwork is a hassle to keep clean." I'm forming a real dislike for the man.

"Oh, Antonio, stop that. You love this house as much as I do," Candy says with slight strain in her voice. It's obvious this isn't the first time they've had this conversation.

"Either way, it's beautiful," I say.

"Do you see the ghost?" Antonio demands.

I look him in the eye. "Not yet. That isn't how this works."

He doesn't back down. "It doesn't work. I think this whole thing is just ridiculous."

"Antonio, please," Candy begs. Another conversation they've certainly had before. "You know it is real. I've sensed it."

Antonio throws his hands up. "You ladies have fun. I'm going to the other room. There's a game on."

"You can tape the game, hun," Candy says to his retreating back. "This is important."

He doesn't stop.

"No worries," I say. "If there is a ghost we will find it without him." I inwardly want to smack the man. If he's this rude in front of strangers, how does he act when they are alone? I search Candy's face, but she's wearing a strained smiled. "Sorry about him."

"Husbands can be like that," Mickey says, shifting her camera from one hand to the other. "Why don't you tell us what you've been experiencing."

"Okay." Candy looks at the camera. "Will you be filming this?"

"We don't have to film you, we can add it later as a voice-over. It is better if we can see the home owner on camera, though," I say.

Candy smooths her dark hair. "Okay. I can do that."

"Where do you feel the spirit the most? Which room?" Mickey asks.

"The front room, there." Candy walks into the room dominated by the large fireplace. A fire burns low in the grate and the cherubs on either side smile at us. "I feel a presence in this room the most. Often, when I'm on the settee, it's like something sits next to me. It's hard to explain."

The settee in question is an antique, deep red with a floral pattern that looks like hand stitching. The legs are carved wood similar to the rest of the house.

"Wait," Mickey says, raising the camera to her shoulder. "Sit there and say that all again."

Candy sits, uncertainty on her face.

"You'll do fine. Just look at me and tell me what you've felt," I say, standing behind Mickey's shoulder.

"My husband inherited this house a few weeks ago," Candy starts. "Almost as soon as we moved in, I sensed, I don't know, a presence." I nod to keep her talking. "It is hard to explain and my husband thinks I'm nuts. I'd be alone in a room and I'd feel someone staring at me. When I turned to look, there was no one there. I'd walk down the hall and there'd be a patch of cold air that had no reason."

She runs a hand along the floral fabric of the settee. "I feel it most intensely here. Often, when I sit here, I feel like someone is sitting beside me. Sometimes I even feel a pressure against my leg, like someone is leaning on me."

"Do you have any idea who it might be?" I ask, off camera.

Candy raises her eyes to mine. "I don't know. It's just a feeling I get."

The low tingle I've felt since we first arrived begins to grow. "But you have an idea? Is there anything else you can tell us?" I ask, looking around the room.

Candy thinks a moment. "This is going to sound silly."

"I'm sure it's not silly," Mickey says.

"I get the sense that it's a little girl."

I look out the window at the cemetery next door. "I know a little girl ghost that lives in the cemetery."

"Really?" Candy asks. "You've seen a ghost there?"

"I've actually seen a few ghosts there. Cemeteries are good places for sightings. I've seen a little girl named Sarah." I join Candy on the settee.

"So I'm not crazy?"

The tingle in my shoulders grows. "Of course you're not crazy. You're just more sensitive than most." I look around the room again. "Let's see if we can find her."

"What do we do?"

"Just sit there and let's see if it is Sarah here."

I stand and walk around the room. Mickey follows me with the camera. "Sarah, are you there?" I ask the room.

Nothing happens.

"Sarah, it's Rylan. We've talked before. You can come out."

The fire suddenly flares bright and sparks rise up the chimney. "Something's here," I whisper to the camera.

NINE

RYLAN FLYNN

"I see you are here," I say loudly. "Is it Sarah?"

I turn slowly, searching each corner of the expansive room. A gray mist fills the doorway. I point to it and Mickey pans the camera in that direction.

"Do you see that?" I ask.

"I don't see anything, but it is growing colder in here," Candy says in a low voice.

It is colder. Goosebumps climb up my arms. I cross the room to the mist. "Sarah?"

The mist takes form and a small girl with haunted eyes takes shape, her white nightgown bright against the dark behind her.

"She's here. It's her. Hello, Sarah. Nice to see you again."

"Have you seen my mommy?" she asks, her dark eyes wide.

"She's asking if I've seen her mom," I tell the camera. "She's standing right here in the doorway. She's wearing an old-fashioned white nightgown."

"Why are you telling them all that?" she asks.

"Because only I can see you."

Sarah looks from Mickey to Candy and says, "She knows I'm here." Sarah crosses the room, climbs onto the settee.

"I feel her," Candy exclaims. "Is she next to me?"

"She is."

"Are you my mommy?"

"She thinks you might be her mom."

Candy looks at the space next to her. "I'm not your mother, but maybe we can find her," she says gently.

"Will you be my mommy?" Sarah leans against Candy.

"I feel her," Candy says.

"She's leaning against your leg," I say breathlessly. The image is heartbreaking.

"Oh, honey, I wish I could help you."

Sarah looks up at Candy. "You're nice. I like you."

"She likes you," I tell Candy. "Keep talking to her."

"Where do you live?"

"Here. I live here. Want to see my room?"

I tell them what she said and Candy looks at me with a question in her eyes. I nod.

"I'd love to see your room."

Sarah jumps from the settee and runs toward the intricate, winding staircase. "It's upstairs."

"She wants us to follow her upstairs."

Candy leads us up, Mickey silently filming the whole scene. Sarah stops at the second door on the left and looks at Candy. "This is where I sleep."

"That's the guest room," Candy tells us when I point to the door.

Sarah walks through the door, Candy opens it for us.

The guest room is as beautifully decorated as the rest of the house. A smaller version of the fireplace downstairs fills most of one wall, although there is no fire tonight. A four-poster bed with a blue and yellow quilt dominates the room.

Sarah turns to me, her face pinched. "This isn't my bed."

"No, it's not," I say as gently as possible.

"Where's my bed? And my toys? My toys are not here."

I tell the camera what she said, her confusion tearing at my heart. "Sarah. You don't live here anymore."

She snaps her head in my direction. "Liar. I live here." She stomps her little bare foot. "I sleep in this room. I play in this room. Mommy?"

She runs to the door and shouts down the hall.

I tell the camera what she's doing.

"Sarah, it's okay. We can get you more toys," Candy says.

Sarah turns on her, her hands balled into tiny fists. "I don't want new toys. I want my mom." She beats against Candy's legs, her fists going right through her.

Candy steps back. "What's going on?"

"She's hitting your legs. She's very upset. She doesn't want new toys." I crouch in front of Sarah. "It's not nice to hit. Now stop that." Sarah stops trying to pound Candy. She stands, panting.

"What's going on? I don't understand. I'm scared." Her face is so pale and her eyes are shadowed.

"What's the last thing you remember from when this was your room?"

She scrunches her face, blinks at tears. "I don't know. I don't want to play with you anymore." She runs into the hall.

I follow, but she disappears.

I turn back to the camera. "She's gone."

Candy walks into the hall. "Sarah, come back."

Heavy footsteps pound up the stairs. "What is going on up here?" Antonio bellows.

"We saw her. The ghost is a little girl named Sarah," Candy says.

"Turn that camera off. This is ludicrous." He raises a hand toward Mickey's lens. I prepare to intervene, but Mickey lowers the camera and Antonio steps away from her.

"We were invited here," I point out.

"Not by me," he grumbles. He looks at Candy's sad face. "I think it is time for you to go."

"Antonio, they are just doing what I asked them to do. And we saw her. She was here."

"You saw the ghost?" He obviously doesn't believe her. "What did she look like?"

Candy hesitates. "Well, actually, Rylan saw her, I didn't."

He glares at me. "Of course you didn't. Now, you two charlatans need to leave."

"We are not charlatans. Sarah was here," I state firmly.

"I don't care." The venom in his voice makes me flinch.

"Let's go," Mickey says, pulling on my sleeve. "We have what we need."

"Enjoy your little show," he says.

I glare at him, but Mickey is pulling me down the steps.

"Thank you," Candy calls after us. "Thank you so much."

"Come on, Candy. It's late and time for bed."

We let ourselves out the front door onto the wide porch. "That went well," Mickey says sarcastically.

I look over to the cemetery, hoping to see Sarah. "It did until he came upstairs."

"Except the part where Sarah ran away."

I shrug. "You know as well as I do, sometimes that happens."

Mickey sighs. "What are we going to do about it?"

I look over the cemetery again, but no Sarah.

"I don't know. She's here for a reason. Maybe if we figure out what the reason is, we can help her cross over to her real mom."

"I don't think we're going to be invited back here," Mickey points out.

"We'll figure something out. We always do." We climb into my car. "Man, he was irritating," I say with a nervous chuckle.

"I thought he was going to lose it when he called us charlatans."

"We've been called worse."

"Unfortunately. At least we have a show for this week. What do you think happened to Sarah?"

"I don't know. Whatever it is, it can't be good."

Mickey looks at me and says, "Uh huh...?"

"What?" I feign innocence.

"You can't stay away from a mystery. You know you're going to find out, or at least try."

"*Beyond the Dead* is a paranormal investigation show. So I'll investigate."

"That's what I thought," Mickey says, then pulls up an old Prince song on her phone and plays it loud as we drive home.

"Let's go crazy!" I sing loudly. I sink into the customary action of singing after an encounter. As I sing along to Prince, my lips make the words, but my mind is on Sarah.

Why is she still here? What happened to her?

TEN

BESS

Earlier

I can breathe. That's the first thing I think of when I wake. My lungs can still take in air. I'm alive.

Stupid, stupid, stupid.

That's the next thought.

How could I be so stupid as to trust a guy I barely know?

I try to move my arms, my legs. They hurt and feel heavy, but I can move them.

I open my eyes and a little girl with long, unkempt, straw-colored hair kneels before me. Her eyes are huge, with dark smudges below them on her very pale skin. One chunk of her hair pokes out above her ear, and bobs as she talks.

"You fell," she says, her voice high and sweet. "Are you okay?"

I push myself to a sitting position and do a mental check. My left shoulder aches more than the rest of me, but I'm all in one piece. My head pounds and I feel something wet dripping down my forehead.

The little girl reaches for the wetness, runs a finger across my forehead. Her finger comes away bright red with blood.

She stares at the blood intensely, then sticks the finger into her mouth.

"Don't," I protest, but she smiles wide, her tongue stained red in the center, that odd chunk of sticking up hair moving as she cocks her head.

I shiver, more afraid of the girl than I am of the man who brought me here and threw me down the stairs.

"Yummy," she says. She suddenly grows serious. "What's your name?"

I try to slide away from the girl, but my back presses painfully into the stairs.

"I'm Missy, who are you?" she says more forcefully.

"I'm Bess," I say.

"Bess, can I call you Mommy? Daddy said he would be getting a new mommy and you must be her."

I shiver with repulsion. I don't want to be this strange girl's mom.

"Where are we?" I look behind me, up the stairs. At the top is a metal trap door.

"We are at home, silly. Where else would we be?"

"This is not my home," I say and scramble up the stairs to the trap door. I know it will be locked, but I try to open it anyway. I bang and pound at the metal door for minutes, but it barely even rattles.

"That's not going to work, Mommy," Missy says, oddly calm. "There's nothing beyond that door. Everything we need is here." She spreads her arms wide and twirls in a circle. "Want to see my room?"

I sit near the top of the steps, rubbing my sore shoulder. I focus on the pounding in my head. "I don't want to be here. I want to go home."

"This is home, Mommy."

"Don't call me Mommy," I snap, sinking onto the steps. "I'm no one's mommy."

Missy smiles again, one side of her lips higher than the other. "Come see my room," she says softly. "And then I'll show you yours."

I have no way of getting out from the stairs, so I descend. At the bottom of the steps, I look around the room. It's like a house, but there are no windows. A couch and a TV are on one side and a small kitchenette is on the other. One whole wall is full of canned goods and supplies.

"Is this a bunker or something?" I ask, dumbfounded.

"We have cookies," Missy says, full of excitement. She hurries to a shelf and pulls down a sealed package. She digs in a drawer for scissors, then cuts the plastic open and takes out a crumbling cookie. She holds it out for me. I take it with weak fingers.

She shoves one in her mouth. "Chocolate chip," she says around a mouthful. "Try it."

I don't want the cookie, but her eyes grow hard and cold. "Try it," she demands in a voice so hard I can't believe it comes from that adorable face.

I put the cookie in my mouth. It is dry and tasteless. I'm suddenly very thirsty.

I do my best to chew and swallow.

Missy grins her lopsided grin. "Good isn't it?"

"It is," I lie.

"Oh, Mommy. You shouldn't lie." She tosses the bag of cookies across the room. "They are horrible," she shouts. The sudden change startles me.

I stare at the girl in confusion.

"Where is your dad?" I ask, not knowing what else to say.

"Oh, he comes and goes. He's gone right now." She looks around the room as if he will suddenly appear in the bunker. "Want to see my room?"

I follow her through a door into a small room. There's a twin-size bed with a purple frilly comforter. And toys. More toys than I've ever seen for one child.

"Do you like it?" Missy asks.

"I do. It's very pretty. You like the ocean?" The walls are covered with posters of the beach, of waves, palm trees, and sand.

"I've never been. Daddy was supposed to take me, but that was before."

"Before what?"

Her lopsided grin sends chills down my back.

ELEVEN

RYLAN FLYNN

Snuggled in my cocoon of a bedroom after our encounter with Sarah, I can't sleep. My body is tired, but my mind won't stop racing.

I think of Sarah and of Bess.

Poor little Sarah, confused and alone.

Poor Bess, missing and hopefully safe. I can't help Bess, but I might be able to help Sarah.

She's still here for a reason. My middle-of-the-night mind thinks it can figure it out. Most likely, Sarah is still here for the same reason as most spirits. To tell how she died.

Did the young girl die under suspicious circumstances?

I throw the blankets off and wriggle to the edge of my mattress.

"I can't sleep anyway," I tell the many stuffed animals staring at me in the dark.

I pull on my Converse sneakers and dig a jacket out of a pile of clothes.

It's a short drive to the cemetery. The lovely Victorian house is dark at this hour, Candy and Antonio presumably asleep inside. Dad's church stands guard. The tall steeple blocks the moon, casting a large shadow across the graves.

It takes me a moment to get my bearings. Years ago, back when I first saw Sarah, I searched out her headstone. Now I need to find it again.

It's at the end of a line of graves, near the Victorian. A small angel sits atop a rectangle of granite. Engraved is her name, *Sarah Carrillo*, and the dates, *April 1, 1881–March 22, 1888*. Sarah was just shy of seven years old when she died. Why hadn't I made the connection of Candy and Antonio's last name being the same as Sarah's?

I run my fingertip over the worn engraving, a deep weight in my heart.

"Such a waste of a life," I whisper. "I'm sorry, Sarah." The angel looks on with her eternally sad expression. A stray leaf blows across the grave, turning in the slight breeze. It lands on the grave next to Sarah's.

There, *Carrillo* is engraved at the top of the larger slab of granite. Below that are the names William and Diana with birth and death dates.

Sarah's parents.

I bend closer to see the dates. Both her father and her mother died a few months before Sarah, only days apart.

"That's odd."

"What's odd?" Sarah suddenly says beside me.

"Holy flip, you scared me." I add more gently, my hand to my chest, "Hi there, Sarah."

"You're that lady from before. Why are you here?"

"I came to see you," I say, afraid to scare her away again.

Sarah looks at her grave, her nightgown blowing in the breeze. "That's my name."

"That's right. It is your name."

She turns her pale face to mine. "Why?"

The pain in that one syllable is potent.

"I was hoping you could tell me. Do you remember before you came to the cemetery?"

"Only dead people are in the cemetery."

I take a moment to form a response to that. How do you explain life and death to a six-year-old? "Do you know anyone that died?"

Her face sags. "Mommy and Daddy died, didn't they? Uncle Ralph brought me here to see their gravestone. It's right there."

"I saw that. It's a lovely spot. Do you remember what happened to your mom and dad?" I push.

She looks at the ground. "They got sick."

"Oh, Sarah, that's awful. I'm so sorry."

She kicks at a pebble. "It wasn't so bad," she lies, trying to be strong. "Uncle Ralph said they went to heaven. He said heaven is a nice place."

"Heaven is a nice place." I stare at her tiny form. "Sarah, do you know what kind of sick they were?"

She shakes her head, her hair covering her pinched face.

"Did they cough a lot? Did they have fevers?"

She lifts her head. "They had pain. I wasn't allowed to go to their room, but I could hear Mommy crying in pain." She sniffles. "I wanted to see them, but Uncle Ralph wouldn't let me."

I'm starting not to like this Uncle Ralph. "That wasn't right. I'm sorry he kept you away."

"Even after they died, he didn't let me see them. I just wanted Mommy." She begins to grow upset.

I try to keep her calm. "I'm sorry, Sarah, but I need you to be a big girl now and try to remember."

She wipes at her nose with the back of her hand and nods. "Remember what?"

"Did you get sick, too?"

She studies the grass, but nods.

"Did anyone tell you what kind of sick you were?"

"They said I had the fever."

"Do you know what a fever is?"

"It's when you get really hot. I had one before. I remember because it was at Christmas and I had to stay in my bed. I was very hot all over."

"Were you hot this time?"

"No, I just had a bad belly ache. It really hurt." She sniffles again.

"Who told you that you had the fever? The doctor?"

"A doctor never came. Uncle Ralph took care of me."

I grow somber. "Sarah, did Uncle Ralph tell you anything you remember? Anything odd?"

She wipes at her nose again and thinks a moment. "Like what?"

"About you going to heaven, maybe."

"Oh, that. Yeah he told me I would soon see Mommy and Daddy." She looks around the cemetery. "Have you seen my mommy?"

"I haven't seen her. I'm sorry."

"Mommy?" she calls across the graves. "Mommy where are you?" Her voice fills with fear. "I'm scared to be alone. Where are you?"

"*Shh*, Sarah," I coo. "You're not alone. I'm here with you."

"Will you stay with me? I'm scared."

"I'll stay." I sit and lean against her headstone. "Here, sit with me."

She lowers her tiny body to the ground, snuggles against my side. I feel a slight pressure where she touches me.

"I'm so cold," she says. "Keep me warm."

"I wish I could. I wish I could."

I sit in the dark and try not to look around the cemetery. I feel other spirits, faint tingles across my shoulders. I don't look. I focus on Sarah.

I lean my head against the cool surface of her headstone,

making myself as comfortable as possible. Sarah wiggles against me. "I like you," she says. "You hear me when I talk. The other mommy never hears me."

Sarah spends the night talking about her life with her parents. She tells me about all her toys, about the dog she had, about the swing in the backyard.

I drift asleep listening to her sweet voice.

TWELVE

FORD PIERCE

I sit on the small patio of my apartment, staring into the abyss of shadows. The breeze makes my arms break out in goose bumps, but I don't go back inside. I need sleep, but my brain won't let me. I sip the beer I opened over an hour ago, hoping it will relieve some of my tension.

The pressure of the cases nearly suffocates me.

Where is Bess?

What happened to Melanie?

How can I solve both cases when I have nothing to go on?

I turn over the few details I have.

Both women disappeared from bars. Are they connected? Lots of women disappear after meeting men in bars.

Except Melanie was there with her sister, and they were different bars. It's a tenuous connection.

I stare at the clouds, agitated and annoyed, and take another sip of my flat beer.

Maybe I should try to sleep.

My mind drifts to the old church. It skitters over Rylan talking to someone I couldn't see.

It is real, right?

It felt real.

Everything with Rylan feels real.

I shove that thought away quickly. Rylan is like a little sister to me. That's all.

I train my mind to think of Bess. I need to find her before something bad happens to her. She has to be found safe. Whoever took her has had her for days.

My phone rings, vibrates in my pocket.

Rylan?

I tell myself that's stupid. She's not calling me.

I sit down my beer and reach for the phone.

It's Kaitlyn.

"Hello?" I ask, guarded.

"Are you awake?" I can tell she's been crying.

"I am." I sit up taller in the patio chair. "You okay?"

"No. I'm not," she sniffles. I give her a moment to get control.

"What happened?"

"Nothing happened. That's the problem. Where is she, Ford? Where is my cousin?"

"I don't know, but I'm trying to find her."

"Are you?" The angry edge in her voice grates my nerves and I remember why we broke up.

"What does that mean?"

"Are you doing everything you can? Seems to me, you're busy playing ghost hunter with that girl and not looking for Bess."

"How do you know about that?" A mixture of guilt and violation fills me. Who has she been talking to? Tyler? Keaton?

"Doesn't matter how I know. I can tell by your reaction that I'm right."

"Kaitlyn, are you following me?"

"I have better things to do than follow you, and you have

better things to do than traipse around an old church with that freak."

"She's not a freak. She's helping with the investigation."

"Whatever." She takes a deep breath. "Just find Bess," she pleads. "Find her before it's too late."

"I'm trying," I say lamely.

"Try harder, Ford." With that, she hangs up on me.

Frustrated, I toss the phone on the patio table.

I want to tell her she's wrong, but can I? Are we doing everything we can to find Bess?

I rack my brain for another angle to look at, another lead to chase. I don't have anything. It's like she walked out of that bar and disappeared.

Is she even still alive?

"Please, Lord, let me find her alive," I say to the night. "Send me a sign of where she might be."

I'm not sure God hears my prayer, but I repeat it over and over as I down the rest of my beer.

THIRTEEN

RYLAN FLYNN

"Things must be going badly if you're sleeping in a cemetery." My brother, Keaton's, voice penetrates the darkness of sleep.

My eyes blink open to the morning sun. I sit up and stretch my neck, stiff from sleeping against Sarah's gravestone.

Sarah.

I look around us in the morning light. "Is she still here?" I ask uselessly. Even if she was, Keaton wouldn't see her.

"Who?"

"The ghost of Sarah Carrillo."

Keaton points to the stone marker behind me. "That Sarah Carrillo?"

"Yeah. She was here last night." I climb to my feet on achy legs. "She's just a little girl and I think she was murdered."

Keaton runs a hand across his face. "It's too early to talk about a murdered girl. Barely even had coffee yet." He holds two cups of takeout coffee with the green The Hole logo.

"You brought me coffee?"

He looks at the cups. "Uh, no. I had no idea I'd find you here. I came to have coffee with Dad. I'm early."

I didn't know Keaton and Dad had coffee together. To be

honest, I don't know much about Keaton's daily life. "That sounds nice," I say lamely, brushing grass off my rear. Dad's car pulls into the parking area. "I wanted to talk to him too."

"About helping this Sarah cross over?" Keaton asks, handing me one of the coffees.

I blink in surprise and reach for the offered cup. "Yes. I need to find out what happened to her first."

Dad walks up the sidewalk, a beam of genuine happiness on his face. "What a lovely surprise," he says. "Both of my kids together. A good way to start the day. You're joining us for coffee, Rylan?"

He looks from me to Keaton and back.

"I kind of slept here last night," I tell him.

The happy grin fades into concern. "Why? What's wrong?"

"Nothing's wrong. Let's go inside and I'll tell you all about it." I look to Keaton for confirmation.

I follow my brother and Dad into the church, looking over my shoulder for Sarah.

We settle in Dad's office and I tell them all about talking to Sarah at Candy's house, leaving out how Antonio basically kicked us out. They both listen intently as I continue to tell them what Sarah said last night.

"So I think her Uncle Ralph killed the whole family," I finish.

"Why would he do that?" Dad asks.

"Probably to get the house and property. Back then, that house was probably the most expensive in Ashby," Keaton says.

"That's what I was thinking." I nod along with my brother.

"What does that mean for Sarah now?" Dad asks.

"I think once we figure out exactly what happened to her, we can help her cross over."

He leans on the desk. "You think she will go? She's been here over a hundred years."

"She's looking for her mom. She doesn't want to be here," I say.

"All of this happened so long ago, what does it matter now?" Keaton asks, always the rational one.

"It matters to Sarah. Her little soul is stuck," I say.

"So what do we do?" Dad asks.

I look at Keaton. "Can we look into the records from that long ago? Maybe see who was to inherit the property before William and Diana died?" As an attorney with the DA's office he has a lot more access than I have. "If you get the records, I will go through them."

"It shouldn't be too hard. They should be in the archives, down at the courthouse. I can show you where to look and you could find them pretty easily."

"That would be great. Can we do it this morning?"

Keaton smiles the patronizing smile I'm used to, more than this helpful attitude he's had this morning.

"Sure. I don't have a meeting until later." I detect a note of annoyance.

"I really appreciate it." I'm not sure why but I feel the need to apologize. My brother just rubs me that way.

"Seems like you've been busy with crimes this week," Keaton says.

Dad looks up expectantly. "Yes, whatever happened with that missing woman? Did they find her yet?"

"I wasn't just talking about Bess Freeman," Keaton says with concern. "I saw you on the news, in the crowd at the scene where they found those bones. I just want you to be careful."

"I was with Ford when he got the call. Of course I went. Who wouldn't?"

"Curiosity killed the cat," he says curtly. He always does this. Starts off friendly then goes in for the kill. A skill he gained in court.

"If you saw the news, you saw there were lots of us there.

Even Kaitlyn showed up." As I remember, Keaton was upset when Ford broke up with Kaitlyn. I think he secretly had visions of Ford and Kaitlyn married and best friends with him and Sheryl. Ford's breakup ruined that happy dream.

"I saw her, too."

"What does it matter who was there?" Dad asks, confused by Keaton's change of attitude.

"It really doesn't." Keaton shrugs. "As long as Rylan isn't involved in that case too. There's starting to be talk down at the office about how you just happen to be at crime scenes lately."

My face flames. Lindy works at that office. I don't want that woman talking about me. "I have nothing to do with any of these cases. I'm just an innocent bystander curious about what's going on."

"So you didn't take Ford to an abandoned church recently?"

"You know about that?" Darn him for making me feel like I have something to hide. "How did you find out?"

"Ford told me this morning. He wanted to know what to do with the information since it wasn't attained in the usual, legal, way."

"I can talk to a murder victim after the fact. That has to be something helpful."

"Wait, what happened?" Dad intervenes.

I tell him about meeting Miss Melanie and how the bones that were found most likely belong to her.

"They confirmed it late yesterday afternoon," Keaton says. "The bones are from Melanie Shaw. Dental records proved it."

"So I was right."

"The dental records are admissible in court. What you found out isn't."

"Always thinking of work," I bristle.

"When it comes to putting a murderer away, yes, I am."

"Then we are on the same team."

"Not exactly. Ford will be a laughing stock if he pursues this 'ghost of the victim' angle. Everything he investigates will be tainted."

"So you're worried about Ford's reputation?"

"I'm worried about you, too. It's one thing to make your little show and to solve a possible murder from a century ago. It's quite another to mess up a case against a current murderer on the loose."

I find myself panting in anger, unable to form a response. My *little show*? How dare he!

"Let's just calm down now," Dad says. "We were having a nice morning visit. Why can't you two just get along? You'd think after your mother—"

We both stare at Dad, then look away. I, for one, feel ashamed at getting him upset.

"I can get along fine," I say as calmly as I can. "It's him that's the problem. Always demeaning what I do. What we do for the spirits."

"I don't mind what you do for spirits. Just stay away from crime cases," Keaton says tightly.

"They come to me. I don't go looking for them. Miss Melanie deserves justice."

"And we will get it for her, the correct way. We don't need you threatening victims."

"Threatening? I didn't threaten her."

"What would you call it?"

"We were just questioning her a little."

"And she called out for help. I'm telling you, this is a dead end."

We stare at each other in silence. The same way we did as kids when we fought over whose turn it was to play Zelda on the Nintendo.

Dad is used to calming us down, distracting us. "Why don't you guys just agree to disagree for now and go look into Sarah's case? Find out what you need to set her free."

I don't look away from my brother. "Can you stop giving me a hard time?"

"Can you stop looking into the Melanie Shaw case and leave it to the police?"

"Agreed."

"Fine. Let's go to the archives." He takes his jacket from the back of his chair and pulls it on. "You might want to wash your face. You have graveyard dirt on your chin."

I want to smack him, but Dad gives me a warning look. "This is a church, Rylan. Be good."

I smile sweetly at Dad and kiss him on the cheek. "I'm always the good one."

FOURTEEN

RYLAN FLYNN

I wish I had time to stop by the house and freshen up a bit. The leggings and sweater I put on late last night are not really proper attire for the courthouse, especially with dirt and grass smudged on one knee. I won't take the time now. If Keaton is willing to help me this morning I don't want to wait. I agree to meet him in the lobby in a few minutes.

I find a parking spot in the town square. The delicious smell of donuts from The Hole wafts across the lawn. My stomach growls and I make a mental note to stop by and see Aunt Val when I'm done.

The courthouse is mostly deserted this early in the morning. A security guard watches as I walk through the metal detector and waves me ahead.

"Have a good morning," he says, barely looking at me. He then does a double take. "You're that ghost hunter," he says.

"I'm Rylan Flynn," I say, holding out my hand. "Nice to meet you... Stan," I read his name tag.

He looks around the deserted lobby, leans close, and says in a low voice. "I've seen all your shows. You're the real deal, aren't you?"

"What you see on our show actually happens, if that's what you mean."

He looks around again. "Are there any, you know, here now? Sometimes I get the feeling I'm being watched."

I don't like being put on the spot like this, but Stan's open smile and friendly energy sucks me in. I make a show of checking out every corner of the lobby. "I don't see anything," I tell him.

He seems disappointed.

"They could just not be here right now," I tell him.

This seems to brighten his mood. "I know there's something going on around here," he whispers. "I even hear footsteps when no one is around sometimes." He flicks his eyes to the wide marble staircase at the far end of the lobby.

I look at the stairs along with him. A tiny tingle niggles at the edge of my consciousness. When I look up, I see a shadow move at the top of the stairs. I make a small sound of surprise.

"What is it?" Stan asks. "You see something, don't you?" He follows my gaze and stares. "I feel it. That sense I'm being watched."

Footsteps creep across the marble lobby floor and Stan grabs my hand. "Do you hear that?"

"What is taking you so long?" Keaton says, coming around the corner. He looks pointedly at Stan's hand on mine. "What's going on, Stan?"

"She saw a spirit," Stan says, dropping my hand.

I give Keaton an apologetic look, but he's not in the mood.

"Here? There are no spirits here," he says with a finality only an attorney can pull off.

"Actually," I begin, then catch Stan's expression. He wears a mixture of excitement with a large dose of fear. "I might be wrong. It was just a moving shadow. It could be the lights."

Stan seems disappointed, Keaton seems mollified. "Okay, then. Now that that's cleared up, can we get to the archives?"

"I still love your show," Stan calls after me as I follow Keaton across the lobby.

Keaton shakes his head in disgust.

"You just hate that I'm almost kind of famous. At least around Ashby."

The clipped sound of shoes on marble is his response.

"The archives are down here," he says after several steps.

"Great." I keep step with him, my sneakers squeaking softly on the polished floor.

He looks down at my noisy shoes and shakes his head.

A thick wooden door, with *Archives* etched on a frosted glass pane, fills the end of the hall.

"We should find what we need in here," he says. I don't miss that he said "we." He pushes on the heavy door and the smell of paper fills my nose.

Shelves of books fill the center of the room. File cabinets line the walls. The room is packed to the ceiling and it's a bit overwhelming.

"Where do we start?" I ask, in awe.

"First we need to find the abstract for that property. It should list all the owners, at least the historic ones. The newest records are kept digitally."

I run my hands along some leather spines on the shelves. "There's so many books. How do you know which are the abstracts?"

"I had to do a property search for a case not too long ago. The book we need should be over here." I follow Keaton to the far corner of the room. Thick books line a shelf, each with an address either embossed on the spine or written on in pen.

I search the addresses for the Carrillo's house. Before too long, I find the book in question.

I pull the heavy book from the shelf and find a table to sit it on. "There's a lot in here," I say. "What is this book, exactly?"

"An abstract is a collection of all the legal documents and

transactions for a property. That house is old, so the oldest transactions are in this book. It should show the transfer of ownership from the dad."

"William," I interject.

"Right, from William to Sarah and then to Ralph. We can at least confirm that part of your theory."

I flip the book open and scan a few pages. It's filled with handwritten records. I'd expected a few legal documents, but there's a lot more.

"This will take a while to go through," I say, reading a passage here and there.

"Take your time. You can stay as long as you need."

I sink into a chair at the work table and look up at my brother. "Thank you."

"No problem," he says.

"No. I really mean it. Thanks for believing in Sarah and her case," I say sincerely.

"As long as it keeps you away from current cases." He ruins what could have been a tender exchange.

"Right," I say tightly.

He studies my face. "You know I just want you safe, Rylan."

"You have a strange way of showing it."

"Have you already forgotten what happened just a few days ago?"

"I haven't forgotten. I just don't want to dwell on it."

"Well, I haven't forgotten, either. We could have lost you." He looks away, down a row of shelves.

"I'm right here. I'm not going anywhere."

He won't look at me for a moment, fiddles with his tie. "Well, okay then. Let me know if you need anything else."

He turns and hurries from the room.

I look after him with a smile. My brother may talk tough and drive me crazy, but, once in a while, he redeems himself.

An hour later, I've found all the information I need. The property did indeed pass to Sarah, with her uncle as the executor until she was of age. According to the book, the property would pass to Ralph in the event of Sarah's death.

Death certificates for William, Diana, and Sarah I find in another part of the archives. All of their causes of deaths were listed as "unknown."

I suspect poisoning from what Sarah told me.

But what can I do with that information? Should I tell Sarah she was murdered? Should I tell Candy and Antonio? According to the records, the house passed down the generations until it was recently left to Antonio. Uncle Ralph was his great-grandfather. Sarah is his relation.

I sit at the table, listening to the silence, when my phone rings and I nearly jump out of my chair.

It's Ford.

"I wanted you to know we got the confirmation from the dental records, the bones are the remains of Melanie Shaw."

"I know, Keaton already told me." I shut the massive book before me.

"Oh, well. I just wanted to be sure you knew."

"That's sweet, thank you." I sit back in my chair, wondering why he really called.

"Also..." He pauses. It's not like Ford to beat around the bush like this.

"Yes?"

"We talked to Melanie's parents this morning. We confirmed she did work occasionally in the daycare at Unity Church in Brighton."

"Ford, are you trying to ask me something?"

A beat of silence.

"I am, but I don't know how to say it."

"Just tell me."

"Tyler wants to talk to Melanie."

"He believes me?"

"We both do. The problem is, anything you find out would be inadmissible in court. We're a little worried the whole thing could come back to bite us if it gets out what we're doing."

"What else do you think Melanie could tell us? She totally shut down last time."

"Maybe it will go better if I'm more careful this time."

I rub a charm from my bracelet in thought. "Maybe."

"Will you do it?"

"I'll have to ask the Stinsons if we can come again," I hedge.

"Without telling them the police are involved."

"Maybe Mickey could come as a cover. I could say we just need to get more footage."

"You're not going to use Miss Melanie as a show are you?"

"No. Not while there's an open investigation."

"Good. That's good. When do you want to do this?"

"No time like the present." My stomach growls loud in the silence of the archives. "I need to run over to The Hole real quick first. I'll call the Stinsons. I'm sure they won't care."

"Set it up and let me know."

"It's a date."

I regret the words as soon as I say them, so I hang up.

FIFTEEN

RYLAN FLYNN

After finishing up at the archives, I follow the lovely smell of pastries across the road to The Hole. The bell jingles overhead as I enter. Aunt Val smiles brightly from behind the counter when she sees me.

"Rylan, what a nice surprise."

"Hey, Aunt Val." She reaches into the display case, grabs a bear claw, and hands it to me.

"Usual?" she asks.

"You know it." I take a big bite of the soft confection. Cinnamon sings on my tongue.

"You're up and around early," she says.

I brush a crumb from my jacket. "I had an interesting night." I look around the store. Only Eileen is in the back and I don't think she can hear me, so I tell Val about Sarah's visit and my sleeping arrangement.

"You have a strange job," she says with a shake of her head.

"It's gotten stranger lately. I've been requested by Ford to do a visit with a ghost out on Knopp Road." I tell her about Melanie.

"Another murder victim? Can't you talk to any ghosts that are happy?"

"If they were happy they wouldn't still be here."

I take another big bite of the bear claw as the overhead bell jingles, and choke when Lindy Parker enters. Her eyes narrow when she sees me.

"Rylan," she says stiffly.

I try to swallow, but a bit has gone down the wrong pipe. I cough out chewed dough all over Lindy's jacket. I continue coughing, unable to stop, as Aunt Val comes around the counter.

She beats on my back. "Just breathe."

I try to take in a breath as Lindy wipes at her chest. "Yuck. Look what you did. You really are a piece of work," she says with disgust.

Val jumps to my defense. "Haven't you ever choked?" she demands of Lindy.

She doesn't comment, just takes napkins from the dispenser on the counter and cleans herself up.

"Sorry," I gasp. "It went down the wrong pipe." I pat my chest and cough again, my eyes watering, feeling like a total fool.

Lindy dabs at her jacket, brushing bear claw onto the floor. "Can I get an Americano coffee?" she asks Val, turning her back on me.

As Val goes back behind the counter, I cough again, but no crumbs fly out this time. "I'll catch you later," I tell Val and slink out the door.

"What does Ford hope to learn by talking to Miss Melanie again?" Mickey asks as she collects the camera in her office.

"I'm not sure. But Keaton won't be happy. He made it very

clear he wants me to stay out of it. He's afraid that anything we learn will not be admissible when we catch her killer."

"And he's right."

"I know. But if we got a clue that led us to actual evidence, that would be good."

Mickey shrugs. "If she's even there."

"Yeah, I wondered about that, too. We can only try."

"I'm surprised that Tyler wanted this."

"Maybe he's secretly a fan." I can barely get the sentence out before I break into a laugh, picturing straight-laced Tyler watching a ghost-hunter show.

"Stranger things have happened." Mickey puts the last item in her bag and zips it closed.

"Speaking of strange things, I saw Sarah again last night." As we leave her house and drive to the abandoned church, I tell Mickey everything I found on Sarah's story. "I'm pretty sure she was murdered, but I don't know how to prove it."

"Or what you could do about it. I mean, it was a really long time ago."

"I'm hoping that once the truth is out, Sarah can cross over."

"The poor thing must be scared. I'm glad she's had Candy for a little while."

"I think we need to contact Sarah's mother and hope she can help her daughter cross over."

"Like a séance?" Mickey asks.

"I don't know. Maybe?" I look at her sideways.

Mickey looks at me with a touch of wonder.

"What?" I ask.

"Did you ever think we'd be doing this?"

"Doing what?"

"When we were kids and you first told me about your gift, I never imagined we'd have *Beyond the Dead*, let alone be part of murder investigations." She pats me on the knee. "It's just cool, how far we've come. I love our little team."

I'm touched by her kind words. "I couldn't do this without you," I say honestly.

"You don't need me to see the ghosts."

"I need you behind the camera for the show and behind me for the rest of it. You've been a good friend and business partner."

"Now stop getting all mushy," she says, her cheeks turning pink. She gives me a warm smile, then changes the subject. "Now, what's the plan with Melanie?"

"I'm not sure what Ford is hoping to find out. She doesn't even realize she's died. So I can't just ask 'Do you remember who killed you?' and solve the case."

"They probably think you can do that."

"I wish."

Ford's personal car, a black Malibu, is parked in front of the old church, and he and Tyler are waiting on the stone front steps.

Tyler shifts his feet uncomfortably when Mickey and I approach. Understandable as we are entering a confirmed haunted house.

"Thanks for doing this, Ry," Ford says. I glow a little at his use of my nickname.

"No problem. Tyler, you remember my friend, Mickey."

He looks at the camera and his eyes grow wide. "You're going to film this?"

"It's more just in case the Stinsons are watching. I told them we were doing some more filming." Tyler looks across the field to the Stinsons' house and takes a step to the left so the church blocks any view of him.

"Don't worry," Mickey says. "I won't get you in the frame."

"Why don't we get started," Ford says, walking up the steps. "Are you feeling anything? Do you think she is here?"

I start up the crumbling stone steps once more and listen to the beyond. "I'm not getting any of the tingles or sensations that

I often get when a spirit is near, but that doesn't necessarily mean anything."

Tyler looks at me seriously. "Is this going to work?"

"Depends on what your definition of working is." I explain the difficulty of getting useful information from Miss Melanie when she won't even accept that she's dead, that getting a name or a description from her is likely impossible.

Tyler's sinking shoulders tell me that's exactly what he had in mind.

"Let's just see how it goes. She might give away some clue and not even know it."

For the third time in two days, I enter the abandoned church.

Mickey has the camera on and is panning around the falling-down space. She'll use these shots as B-roll for the show. If we ever get to make this episode.

Tyler looks up at the sagging ceiling of the sanctuary. "Is it safe in here?"

"Probably not," Ford says. "But that never stops Rylan."

We wait a few minutes while Mickey does her thing, then I lead us down the stairs.

"Phew, the smell is bad here," Tyler says.

"I think it's grown worse since yesterday," Ford says. He meets my eyes, no doubt remembering a similar smell we both found recently.

"A dead animal?" Mickey asks.

"Maybe," Ford says, unconvinced.

"It seems to be coming from over that way," Tyler says, all business now. He's familiar with the smell of death, too. This is very similar.

At the far end of the meeting area is a short hall that leads to the bathrooms. Ford and Tyler take the lead and I follow closely. Mickey films us, obviously forgetting her promise not to put the police on film.

We creep down the tiny, shadowed hall. "It's strongest here," Ford says in a low voice, pointing to the men's room door.

Tyler places a hand against the swinging door and pushes it open.

A wave of horrible smell pours out.

Mickey is close behind me. "What is it?"

I put a hand to my nose and peek in, expecting a rotting corpse.

Ford and Tyler enter the cramped space and scan the gloom. There are two stalls, and each open a door.

"Found it," Ford says, backing away from the stall, his hand to his nose.

"Is it a body?" I ask breathlessly.

Ford shakes his head. "No. Well, not exactly." He backs away so I can look in. The toilet is full of a foul, chunky liquid. Some of it has overflowed from the bowl and pooled around the base. The bloated corpse of a large rat lies in the puddle.

I back away from the mess and Tyler looks in.

"Bad plumbing and a dead rat," Mickey says with a nervous laugh. "Phew, I was sure we were going to find something awful."

"That is awful," Tyler says, obviously relieved.

"Let's get out of here," Ford says. He is right behind me in the cramped space. He puts his hand on my elbow and gently presses me toward the door. He is standing so close I can feel the heat of his body against my back.

My body misbehaves and presses into him before I can stop it. I feel his chest muscles against my shoulder blades for a split second. Then my wits return and I step forward.

He lets go of my elbow and I feel a sudden emptiness.

My skin remembers all the places he touched me, each tiny place burning with longing.

Get yourself together.

I notice a different, more insistent tingling. Just then, a banging echoes through the darkened meeting room.

"It's coming from the daycare room," Mickey says, turning the camera on the door.

"I think Melanie is here, after all," I say.

"Get out! I don't want you here," Melanie shouts, followed by the sound of something hitting against the door.

We all jump at the sudden crash. "She's telling us to leave. She doesn't want to talk to us."

"Have you had this happen before?" Ford asks.

"Sometimes. The spirits don't always want to be seen."

Another crash makes the door swing open a little.

"What the—" Tyler flinches. "How is she doing that?"

"When they try really hard, ghosts can move things. She must be very upset to be throwing things."

I look to Ford. He seems worried. "Maybe this is a bad idea. I don't want a ghost throwing things at us."

"Go away! I know you are there."

The door suddenly swings open and Miss Melanie crashes into the meeting room.

"She's in the room," I tell the group. "Right in front of the door."

"I don't want you," she cries. "You say awful things."

"Miss Melanie," I soothe, "We don't want to upset you."

She looks down at the dirty floor. "You said I was dead. Do I look dead?"

"You look lovely," I tell her. "We just want to know what happened to you."

"Nothing happened. I was at the bar then I was here."

I tell the group what she said.

"Between the bar and here, what happened?"

Melanie glares at me, her chin stern.

"Will you please tell me?" I ask gently.

"She didn't mean to do it." Melanie hangs her head.

Excited, I take a step closer. "Who didn't mean to do what?"

Melanie's head hangs so low that her hair covers her face. She shakes her head, her hair swinging from side to side.

"I won't tell you. That's personal."

She turns away and moves back to the door. From this view, I can see it.

The stab wound in her back.

SIXTEEN

RYLAN FLYNN

A few minutes later, we pour out into the spring sunshine.

"That was wild," Tyler says. "We actually talked to a ghost."

"It's a rush, for sure," Mickey concedes. "I never get used to it."

"Phew," Ford says. "I told you, Tyler."

The three of them all chatter and laugh, excited by the encounter. I'm filled with a sadness for Melanie. She seems so scared. "She was stabbed to death," I say, shattering the good mood.

Ford grows serious. "How do you know? Did she say so?"

"She said, 'She didn't mean to do it'. And then, when she turned away, I saw the stab wound in her back."

"Wonder who the 'she' is," Ford says. "We know that Melanie disappeared from the Juke Joint after spending time with a man there. We assumed who she left with was who killed her. Does she remember anything else?"

I shake my head. "I don't know. That's all she said."

"Can you go back and ask her?" Tyler asks.

"She won't tell me. I'm sorry."

Ford paces in front of the church, thinking. I remember him

doing this exact thing as kids when he and Keaton were studying in the dining room. He always thinks better on his feet.

"So what do we know?" he asks.

"According to the report from when she went missing, she was last seen at the Juke Joint with a man," Tyler says. "We have the description of the man, but it's vague. Middle-aged white man, average height and weight. Brown hair."

"Not much to go on," Mickey says. "That could be most men in town."

"It also means nothing if Melanie says she was stabbed by a woman."

"Might lead us to the woman if we figure out who the man is," Ford points out.

"Or the man means nothing," I say.

"It's a start," he returns.

"What about the Reed angle?" I ask. "Think there's anything there?"

Tyler puts a hand on Ford's shoulder. Ford realizes he's talking about the case to me and doesn't answer.

"Thank you for your help, Rylan," Tyler says suddenly. "It was a very interesting experience." He hurries to Ford's car.

Ford follows with an apologetic smile.

"That's it?" I call after them.

"Sorry," Ford mouths.

I take a step toward the car, but they have already climbed in and the engine is running.

"It's not worth it," Mickey says gently. "Let them go."

"But I could help them."

"They don't want our help."

"That's what makes me mad," I grumble, walking to the Caddy and climbing in.

Mickey joins me in my car.

I sit and stare at the church steps. "Why do I feel used?" I ask.

"Because you kind of were."

I seethe at being tossed out of the investigation. Although I understand the reasoning, it still makes me angry.

"Let's just go back to my house and we can talk about helping Sarah. Ford and Tyler can't stop you from doing that."

"Good point," I concede. "First, I need to check in with the Stinsons."

The Stinson home is in much better shape than the abandoned church on their property. A two-story farmhouse with green shutters. Mrs. Stinson answers the door, a guarded look on her face and yellow kitchen towel in her hands. "Did you get all the tape you needed?" she asks, glancing over my shoulder at Mickey.

"We did. Thank you for letting us come again," I say.

"I saw another car with you," she says, shuffling her feet. "I thought you were just filming for your show."

"Well," I stall, wondering if she knows the police were here. "I had a few friends come to see the church."

"You mean to show off the ghost. I know that place is haunted." Mrs. Stinson stares at me with sharp intent, tossing the towel over her shoulder. "Did you clear the ghost out yet?"

"Not yet," I say.

"Maybe you should worry about that and not showing off for your friends." She lifts her chin.

I'm surprised at the anger. In my dealings so far with the family, they have been nothing but kind and interested. "I wasn't—" I start.

"We should be done now," Mickey cuts in.

"Good." Mrs. Stinson won't make eye contact with me now. She focuses on my sneakers. An awkward moment of silence fills the front step.

"Mom, where's the remote?" the son calls from inside the house.

Mrs. Stinson begins closing the door. "I hope you got all you needed," she says. It sounds almost like a warning.

The door snaps closed before I can answer.

———

A little while later, Mickey and I are settled in her dining room with cans of root beer. "You guys want some sandwiches?" Marco asks.

My stomach rumbles. I never finished the bear claw after coughing it all over Lindy.

"I'd love one," I tell him.

"You're the best, babe." Mickey beams at her husband. For the thousandth time, I wonder what life would be like with a loving husband and a nice home like this one. I try to picture Ford making Mickey and me sandwiches in my over-crowded house.

I can't make the picture come into focus and that makes me sad.

"Ham okay?" Marco asks.

"Sounds great," Mickey says. "So what do you want to do about Sarah? Were you serious about the séance thing?"

"Not a séance exactly, but I thought maybe we could try to contact her mother to help her cross over."

"Rylan, that's the definition of a séance," Mickey points out. Over her shoulder, in the front room, I see a shifting shadow. The little boy ghost is eavesdropping. Mickey follows my line of sight and looks hard into that room. "You see him, don't you?" she whispers, not wanting Marco to hear there's a ghost in their house.

"I saw a shadow, but it might be nothing," I hedge. "So, back to Sarah. I don't think we are trained to do something like that. Helping Sarah cross over maybe, but not calling her mother back the other way."

Mickey is staring into the front room, trying in vain to see the boy. "Even I can't see him," I whisper. "He's just a moving shadow."

She pulls her attention back to our conversation, a small furrow between her brows. "Who do you think we could get to do it?"

"Do what?" Marco says, sitting our sandwiches down on the table.

"Rylan wants to do a séance to bring that Sarah ghost's mom over to our side."

I expect lots of questions, but Marco obviously got the whole story from Mickey already. Another part of their relationship I am jealous about.

"Ooh, that sounds interesting. Who could do it?" He thinks a moment. "Wait, what about that witch lady that gave you the book?"

I shoot Mickey a look. Does she tell him everything? Mickey just shrugs.

Marco has a point, though. Lorraine the White Witch could probably do something like that. It's at least worth looking into.

"I could ask her," I say.

"We need Candy, too, since Sarah is so connected to her. I'm not sure Antonio will go for that."

"Antonio will just have to get over it." I take a big bite of my sandwich, sinking my teeth into the soft bread.

Mickey smiles. "When do you want to do this?" She takes a bite of her own sandwich.

I swallow. "Sooner the better. First I have to figure out what to do about Uncle Ralph and the murders he committed."

Marco is listening from the doorway to the kitchen. "Well, you guys do have a show. Expose him on that."

"But he's been dead for a hundred years," I say.

"So. Better his name is remembered for the crimes he committed."

"And his descendants know the truth. Maybe it will knock that Antonio down a peg or two," Mickey says.

I nod along. "Let's do it," I say around a mouthful of ham and cheese.

Mickey hands me a napkin. "You call Lorraine and Candy and set it up. Maybe tomorrow?"

I wash down the last of my sandwich with the root beer. "I'll tell Dad. We'll need his help."

"Wish I could see this," Marco says from the kitchen door.

Mickey and I exchange a glance. The shadow has returned in the door to the front room. Mickey catches my look.

"You want to be around ghosts?" Mickey asks Marco.

"Well, not actually." He gives an exaggerated shiver. "It's fun to think about, though."

The shadow in the front room fades and I shake my head at Mickey to tell her he's gone again.

She downs the remainder of her root beer, looks into the front room longingly. She seems like she wants to say something about the shadow I saw, but doesn't. She sets the empty root beer on the table and says. "Let's set it up."

SEVENTEEN

BESS

Earlier

The girl, Missy, refuses to answer my question.

"Why didn't your dad take you to the ocean?" I repeat.

Her smile disappears. "I'll show you your room." She changes the subject, leaving the toy-crowded room.

I follow across the main area to a door on the other side of the stairs. The door is metal with large hinges. It is closed tight. "You'll sleep in here." Missy turns the heavy knob and pushes the door open.

It's completely dark inside with no windows, just like the rest of the rooms. She flips a switch and the room flickers into light.

It looked better in the dark.

This room is smaller than Missy's. A tiny cot is shoved into one corner. Next to it is a scratched dresser with three drawers. The rest of the room is empty. The gray concrete walls and floor are a stark contrast to the rest of the bunker. Outside of this room, some care was given to create the semblance of a home.

Here, everything is stark and cold. A worn blue blanket on the cot is the only comforting touch.

Missy enters the cramped space and sits on the bed. "Do you like it?"

I stand in the doorway, not wanting to enter. "It's okay."

Her face beams. "I told Daddy to get you a new blanket, but he didn't."

"Where is your daddy?" As far as I can tell, Missy's room and this room are the only doors off the main area.

Is he going to sleep in here with me?

"He'll be around."

"Where does he sleep? Is there another room?"

I step back into the main room, checking again for other doors. Shelves line one wall, the kitchenette fills the second, a TV and a shelf of books fills the third, and the stairs are on the fourth. Under the stairs is another door hidden in the shadows.

"Where does this go?" I cross to the narrow door and turn the knob with anticipation.

A miniature shower stall, a little sink, and a toilet fill the room.

"That's just the bathroom." Missy joins me at the door. "Nothing exciting in there."

The sink is full of toothpaste globs and the toilet paper needs changing. The whole room has a scent of mold and mildew.

"It smells," Missy says and pulls the door closed.

I've seen all the bunker has to show me. The rooms seem to move nearer, the air grows staler, the lights dim as a panic attack sets in.

My chest hurts and I gasp for air, panting.

"I can't be here," I beg. "Please let me out."

I sink to the floor as my body floods with unwanted adrenaline. With shaking hands, I pull at the collar of my sweater.

Missy stands over me, a look of disgust on her face. "You're worse than the others."

I snap my head up to look at her. "What others?" I manage, tears squeezing from my eyes.

She smiles. "Never mind that. Stop crying."

My heart thuds painfully in my chest and I can't catch my breath for long moments. I swallow a few times, focus on my breathing like my therapist taught me. She never thought I'd be in this situation, though.

"Where's your dad?" I ask again. I want to get away from this strange girl. "I want to go home."

"I told you this is home. Daddy will come when he wants."

I look up the stairs at the metal trap door. It's locked from the outside. "Why did he lock us in here?"

"Why would we need to leave?" She turns away and walks to the couch. She flops down and fishes the remote from the flattened cushions. "Want to watch cartoons?"

I can't be here.

This can't be real.

Still huddled on the floor, I scream and scream for help.

Missy watches from the couch with an eerie calm.

When I stop to catch my breath, she says. "Can you stop carrying on? No one will hear you."

She turns back to the colorful pictures on the screen, not bothered by my screaming.

I sit on the hard floor a few more minutes, unsure what to do. While she's distracted, I climb up the steps to the trap door. There's no handle or any way to open it from this side. I still bang on it.

I pound until my hands hurt.

"Stop making so much noise," a man's voice says from below me. "You're scaring Missy."

EIGHTEEN

JAMIE BLAKE

Our newest flip project seems to talk to me from the street. Sometimes the houses are like this. They seem to call to me.

This one did the minute I saw the listing. When I showed it to my business partner, Graham, he didn't share my enthusiasm.

"See that roof? It will need to be torn off and replaced," he'd said.

I didn't listen. It's not good to get emotionally attached to a house-flipping project, but this one got to me.

"It's perfect," I say as Graham and I climb the front steps of the covered porch on the first work day. I set my heavy tool box down and fish the keys out of my pocket. "Look at this leaded glass." I run a finger across the window in the door.

Graham seems unimpressed. "It's nice," he says, noncommittally.

"Spoilsport." I don't let him get me down. I'm sure he will love the house as much as I do once we get into it.

"How long did she say this has been vacant?" he asks.

"Only about four years," I say with as much forced optimism as I can muster. Four years is not the longest vacancy time we have worked on, but it does mean the house has been left to rot for longer than I like.

To prove my point, the door sticks when I try to push it. Only when I shove my shoulder against the wood does it pop open. I lose my balance and nearly fall into the house. Graham grabs the back of my t-shirt to balance me.

"Careful, Jamie," he says.

I smile apologetically up at him. "Let's look inside."

The interior is the same as when we came on a showing a few weeks ago. It looks like the previous owners just walked out one day. Everything is in place.

"Jody said the previous owners just left town and never came back. The bank took the house back," I say.

"And now we have it," he says with a touch of regret.

"It will be great," I tell him. "Stop being such a downer."

"The space is good," he concedes. "And I like that window."

"See," I say stepping into the dining room. "We can open this up to the kitchen and it will be a nice, inviting space."

Graham follows me into the kitchen. "This will need to be torn out," he says about the dated cabinets and appliances. "But with a bar here, this could be really nice."

I touch him on the shoulder. "See. Trust me. I have a good feeling about this place."

As we discuss the changes we need to make, I get the feeling someone is watching us. I look over my shoulder. Maybe Jody, our realtor, has stopped by. Or maybe a neighbor saw us come in and wants to say hi.

No one is there.

"What?" Graham asks with concern.

I shake my head. "Nothing, I guess. I just thought someone was here."

Footsteps echo on the stairs.

I look at Graham. "Did you hear that?"

He's inspecting the plumbing under the sink, but looks up. "I didn't hear anything."

I walk into the front room and look up the stairs to the second-floor landing. "Hello?"

Graham is suddenly beside me. "What are you doing?"

"I swear I heard footsteps."

"Stop goofing around, Jamie. There's no one here but us."

The upstairs landing is dim, but I don't see anyone. "Maybe the house is getting to me. It's weird that the family's things are all still here."

"Or maybe it's haunted," Graham teases.

"Stop that." I smack him on the shoulder. "I swear I heard something."

"Ready to get started?" He smiles, handing me a sledge hammer.

"This is my favorite part." I smile back, lifting the hammer.

I aim for the outdated, sagging cabinets. Putting all my weight into it, I slam into the wood.

The cabinet splinters and pieces fly across the room.

"That felt good," I say, beaming at Graham and blowing my bangs out of my face. I take another swing, and hear the satisfying crunch.

Graham has his own sledge hammer and cracks it across the cabinets. More splinters fly.

We take turns hammering the upper cabinets and then take a drink break.

I down a big gulp from my gas station cup of Dr. Pepper. "Want some?"

"No, I'm good." Graham always brings his own huge water bottle. "That stuff will kill you, you know."

"You tell me that almost every day, but I'm still here."

He takes a big swig of his water in answer.

I stand and tuck a stray strand of my long red hair back into its pony tail. "Ready?" I lift my hammer and aim for a lower cabinet. I take a swing and a door flies across the room.

I freeze at what I see inside.

It's a dried body smiling up at me.

"Holy crap," I say, jumping back and dropping my hammer with a thud.

"What's wrong?" He looks into the cabinet.

The human form is unmistakable. "I think it's a woman."

Scraps of denim and the remains of a t-shirt cling to the body. Long blonde hair sticks to the skull. All of the skin is dried and tight. She looks like a mummy.

My stomach heaves.

I run from the kitchen, through the front room. The front door sticks when I pull on it. "Open, you stupid thing," I shout.

"Jamie?" Graham is right behind me.

The front porch creaks as I run across it. A board breaks underneath my foot and I fall through. The wood pokes my shin, cuts into me.

Graham grabs me under the arms and pulls me out of the hole. "It's okay. It's okay," he repeats into my hair.

Over his shoulder, through the open door, I see a shadow shift across the front room. I flinch, and he feels it.

"Shh," he soothes. "We'll call the police and they will handle this."

I realize he is holding me against his chest. We've worked together for years, but have never been like this. I feel my face flame and disentangle myself from his arms.

"I'm okay," I say, feeling foolish. "I just got startled."

I take a deep breath of the fresh air and look around the neighborhood. The houses next door are vacant, as is the house across the street. Everything looks the same as it did when we came onto the property.

I feel different.

"You okay?"

"She's dead. Someone put her into that cabinet and left her there." I shove my shoulders back and try to get control. "Okay, we have to call the police."

I fish my phone out of my jeans and, with shaking fingers, dial 911.

———

Graham and I wait on the front porch for the police to arrive. My hands grip the railing and his lie next to mine, close, only an inch away.

Again, I hear footsteps from inside the house, but I don't turn.

Graham doesn't hear them.

I suddenly hate this house.

What was supposed to be a good investment is now a crime scene.

A tear slips down my cheek.

Graham's hand is half an inch away now.

I slide mine and close the distance.

As sirens sing in the distance, I touch his hand with mine.

There's no one I'd rather have next to me at this moment.

NINETEEN

RYLAN FLYNN

I leave Mickey's with a sense of purpose. I can't help Miss Melanie, but I can help Sarah. I call Candy and get her voicemail. Not sure what to say on the message, I just ask her to call me back.

On my way home, I see a sign for a garage sale. I don't need anything, but I find myself turning as if the car has a mind of its own.

The bear is staring at me as soon as I pull up to the curb. A stuffed bear, at least four feet tall, light blue fur with a pink bow around its neck.

It's horrible and beautiful and completely too large.

I know before I get out of the car that the bear will go home with me.

I try to avoid the bear, look around the rest of the sale and not at the huge stuffed animal. I can feel it watching me.

"I don't need anything," I tell myself. "My house is full enough."

My feet don't agree and I find myself standing in front of the bear, looking at the tag taped to its ear. Only five dollars.

I tell myself no, but wrap my arms around it anyway.

It smells of dust and baby powder. It's soft and squishy and I fall in love instantly.

I fish a five from my purse and pay the lady running the sale.

"Hope you love him as much as my daughter did," the lady says with a sadness that doesn't match the afternoon sunshine.

I don't ask questions. I just hug the bear tighter and walk to the car.

I place the blue bear in the passenger seat next to me. It is so large it takes up the whole space. I debate buckling him in, but decide against it.

As we drive home, I keep looking at the bear with a mixture of awe at how cute he is and disgust that I gave into buying him. I have dozens and dozens of stuffed animals. My house is already packed with items from other impromptu trips to garage sales.

This bear is huge and will take up what small space is left in my room.

I don't care. I had to have him.

As I drive, sirens wail in the distance, coming closer. I check the rearview mirror and see a squad car approaching. I pull over, wondering what I did to garner police attention.

The car passes without another look.

"Wonder where he's going in such a hurry," I tell the bear.

He grins his permanent grin.

Before I pull back into the road, another cruiser passes with its lights on.

Curiosity gets the better of me and I follow the lights.

———

Police vehicles crowd the front of a rundown two-story house in a sad part of town. I see Officer Frazier stringing yellow crime tape between two trees. I park across the street. Frazier spots me and gives a stern look, no doubt annoyed to see me.

A shadow suddenly fills the passenger window.

"Rylan, how did you get here before us?" Ford asks, leaning into the window when I roll it down.

"I just followed the lights."

Ford looks at the bear and tries unsuccessfully to hide a smile. "A gift for someone?"

I want to lie, to tell him it's for a niece. He knows I don't have a niece.

"I saw it at a garage sale. He's cute don't you think?"

"Sure," he says. "Very blue."

"So what happened here?" I quickly change the subject.

He looks at the house, then back at me. "A body was found."

"Another one?" I gasp.

"Looks like it."

I scan the house. Officers mill around the yard and the front porch. A pretty redhead and a man wait next to a tree. "Who's that?"

Ford studies the couple. "Must be the house flippers that found the body."

On the porch is a blonde woman watching the police with interest.

"And on the porch?"

Ford looks, then turns to face me.

"That's just Officer Ramone."

"Not him. The woman. Is she with the coroner's office or something? I don't recognize her."

He looks again. "There isn't a woman on the porch."

I get a sinking feeling, realize the tingle in my belly is not just from Ford's proximity.

"I think I see your victim."

Ford looks at the porch then back to me, excited.

"Really? What does she look like?"

"Blond hair, about five foot eight, slim build. She's looking right at us."

"Wow. I can't see her. Not even a shadow. How do you do that?"

"I don't do anything. She's just there."

I catch Officer Frazier staring at Ford and me. I glare back and he looks away.

In my rearview mirror, I see the black coroner's van pulling up to the scene.

"There's Marrero," I say.

"You better go. He won't like seeing you at yet another scene."

"I'm not afraid of him."

"Well, I am. He's kind of in charge here."

"Good point," I concede.

Ford reaches in and pats the bear on the head. "Enjoy your new friend. Does he have a name?"

"Not yet."

"What about Darby? He looks like a Darby."

My heart melts that he isn't making fun of me about the bear. "Darby it is," I say with a wide smile.

He pats the window sill and waves goodbye.

I smile all the way home.

Once in my driveway, I wrestle Darby out of the front seat and carry him up the walk. I balance him on my hip like a child as I open the front door. When I push the door it only opens a few inches. Something must have fallen in front of it.

"Holy flip," I mutter, pushing and shoving.

The door won't budge.

I hang my head in defeat. The hoard inside sometimes wins.

I shift Darby on my hip, making my way around the house

to the sliding door in the dining room. I push the door open and wriggle past a pile of boxes into the house.

Once inside, I look at my collection of piles, of boxes, of clothes, of knick-knacks, of everything one could imagine.

A deep sense of hopelessness fills me. I really should clean all this out.

But the thought of getting rid of my many treasures scares me. These aren't just things. The piles are protection.

With Darby held out in front of me, I make my way to the hall. I peek inside Mom's room, but she isn't there. I often wonder what she thinks of the crowded house. Does she even know, since she never leaves her room?

The boxes piled in front of Keaton's door make the hall very narrow. Darby won't fit through the gap.

I try different angles. I try lifting him over my head. He won't fit through the space.

I want the bear in my room. Especially after Ford saw him and liked him. It's almost like having a piece of him with me.

I shove Darby between the boxes and the wall.

Boxes tumble off the stack, crashing into the hall.

The thing locked inside Keaton's room awakens and bangs on the door.

I freeze in fear.

It is so close.

The door handle rattles.

"Go away!" I scream at the door, to the thing.

The handle rattles again, the door shakes with the banging.

I'm scared into movement.

With Darby on the other side of the pile, I begin stacking boxes again. As high as I can reach, for at least a foot on either side of the door, I use the boxes to create a barrier.

The banging is muffled, but still clamors.

Once the boxes are in place, I hold the bear close and back into my room, shoving the bedroom door closed behind me.

I can still hear the banging.

"I don't want you here!" I shout.

I climb onto the bed with my arms around Darby. I curl into the corner, pulling the blankets over us both.

"It can't get out," I tell the bear. "It can't hurt us."

A wail echoes down the hall, through my locked door.

"It can't get you," I repeat, shoving my hands against my ears.

Keaton's door rattles and I cower further into the corner of my bed. I pull other stuffed animals against me, hiding behind their fluff.

Darby is wrapped tightly in my arms.

"Go away," I beg. "Please, go away."

The rattling of the door stops.

The wailing in the hall stops.

The house is silent.

I sit with my army of stuffed animals and listen for the thing.

The house is so quiet, I can hear the ticking of the clock.

It's gone. For now.

TWENTY

FORD PIERCE

"What's with the smile?" Tyler asks as I walk to the house after telling Rylan goodbye.

I didn't realize I was smiling and school my face into an expression more fitting to the crime scene.

"Ready to go in?" I change the subject, starting up the front steps.

"Watch that hole," Officer Ramone says, pointing to a broken board. We carefully step over the spot and head inside.

The house is a buzz of activity, most of it centered in the kitchen.

"Back here, Detectives," an officer directs us.

The kitchen looks like a bomb went off. A red-handled sledge hammer lies among the debris of cabinet pieces strewn about.

One lower cabinet is missing its door and is a bit squished. Inside, the remains of what looks like a woman are curled up. Her flesh has shriveled away and her skin is dried and tight across the bones. Her mouth hangs open in a menacing grin.

I pull away from the sight.

"Well, that's something we haven't seen before," Tyler says nervously.

I look back. The body wears jeans and a t-shirt and has long blonde hair.

I expected the blonde hair after what Rylan saw. I didn't expect the well-preserved state of the body.

"How long does it take to turn a body into a mummy?" I ask.

"It's not a mummy," Dr. Henry Marrero states, walking into the kitchen. "What's with this mess?" He looks around the half-destroyed room.

"Why not a mummy?" Tyler asks, ignoring the comment about the mess.

Marrero looks at the woman's remains, then answers Tyler. "A mummy is technically created by being embalmed, like the Egyptians did. This body is desiccated."

His pompous attitude grates my nerves, but I nod along anyway.

"How long does it take a body to desiccate?" I ask.

"Depends on conditions," Marrero crouches before the cabinet. "With this door closed, and the house abandoned, I'd say three years maybe four."

"That's about when the house was abandoned, according to the house flippers."

"Flippers?" Marrero says.

"That's who found her. They were demoing the kitchen so they could re-model the house," Tyler says.

Marrero looks around at the broken cabinets and shrugs with disgust. "Nothing wrong with the kitchen as it is."

Except the dead body under the counter, I want to point out, but I know better than to cross the cranky coroner.

"I saw you talking to your girl when I drove in," he says to me. "She needs to stop showing up at crime scenes and getting in the way."

"She's not *my* girl. She's a friend." I don't know why I feel the need to explain myself. Rylan didn't do anything wrong.

Marrero scrutinizes me and I feel like a little boy getting caught stealing cookies. He raises his eyebrows then turns back to the body, giving an account of what he's seeing to his assistant.

I leave the kitchen with Tyler close behind me.

"Let's look around the house," I say, heading up the steps.

The upstairs is like the rest of the house. It looks like the family that lived here just up and left everything.

One of the rooms obviously belonged to a little girl judging by the purple sheets on the mattress. The room is scattered with a child's belongings. There are books on the dresser and an ugly puppet on a shelf. But some things are definitely missing.

"No comforter or blankets," Tyler points out.

I look around at the empty shelves that must have held toys at one time. "No toys, either."

Tyler opens a drawer on the purple dresser. "All the clothes are gone, too."

When we check what must have been her parents' room, everything is still there, except a few empty drawers in the dresser. All the wife's clothes still hang in the closet and fill her drawers. The empties look like they belonged to the husband.

"Why leave the wife's stuff?" Tyler asks. I motion to the floor, to the kitchen below. "Right. She didn't need them."

"Looks like he killed her, hid her, then ran off with the little girl."

"And only took clothes and toys. Do we know who owned the house then?"

"Won't be too hard to find out."

I notice a photograph on a side table and look at it closely. The woman has long blonde hair like our victim. "Guess this is her." The ornate frame says *Jacob and Lynette forever* and a date of twelve years ago.

"Looks like happiness didn't last forever for them," Tyler says.

"It rarely does." I think of Kaitlyn and how we used to be so happy.

Until we weren't.

"Wonder where Jacob ran off to."

"We'll find him. He has some explaining to do."

"Detectives," a female voice calls up the steps. "He'd like to speak to you."

I have no doubt "he" is Marrero.

Tyler hurries from the room and, when I see the owner of the voice, I understand why. It's the tech he was friendly with when we found Melanie's bones, Marrero's assistant. The tech smiles brightly up the steps when she sees him.

He hesitates, his hand on the rail. "Hi," he says.

I hide a smile and give him a little shove to make him go down the steps.

"Michelle," Tyler says, an unusual softness to his voice. "Good to see you again."

"Good to see you, Detective Spencer."

He leans close, but I can still hear him. "You can call me Tyler."

"Detectives, if you don't mind," Marrero barks from the kitchen.

Michelle smiles an apology and lets us pass.

"We were just upstairs looking around." I hate that I again feel like I need to explain myself. "Do you have something?"

"Just a cause of death, if you're interested," he says sarcastically, looking at Michelle then Tyler with a knowing expression.

"Of course. What did you find?"

"Stab wounds to the chest. You can see them clearly right here and here." He points with a latex gloved hand.

"Stabbed and stashed in a cabinet. That's awful," Michelle says. Marrero gives her a harsh look and she drops her eyes. I don't like the way he's treating his tech, or us, but I have to play nice.

"So, looks like at least two wounds," I say, crouching next to the coroner.

"That's all I've seen so far. I'll know more when we get her to the lab." He pulls off his glove with a snap. "I think I'm done here. You can have her loaded."

Michelle and another tech make the arrangements to have the remains removed. Tyler and I get out of the way.

"What do you want to do now?" Tyler asks.

"First, I want to know who owned this house. The flippers said they bought it from the bank. My money is on the Jacob in that picture upstairs."

"Would be a good assumption." We walk out onto the front porch, avoiding the hole in the floor. The house flippers still stand by a tree nearby. Officer Frazier approaches.

"They want to know if they are free to go or if you need to talk to them again," he says, motioning to the redhead and her companion.

"I'd like to ask them a few more questions," I say, descending the stairs to the weedy lawn.

The female looks shaken and pale, while the man with her hovers protectively. I wonder if they're just business partners or something more. When she sees us coming, her back straightens.

"Detectives, do you need anything else from us? I'd really like to leave," she says, looking at the house with a mixture of fear and awe.

Tyler already got their statements before I arrived, but I want to talk to them myself. "I'm Detective Pierce." I reach out my hand. Her fingers are long and slim, but there's a surprising strength in them.

"I'm Jamie Blake and this is my partner Graham Spalding." The man shakes my hand, too, his palm rough and calloused.

"I'm so sorry you had to see what you saw this morning," I say. "I understand it can be upsetting."

"That's an understatement," Graham says, his hand briefly touching Jamie's back.

"I got startled, but I'm okay now," she says, pulling on the hem of her t-shirt nervously. "What questions do you have for us?"

"Let's start with a walkthrough of everything you've done here, things you might have touched, that kind of thing."

"That's easy. We really didn't touch anything except in the kitchen."

"I looked under the sink at the plumbing. Then we started demoing the cabinets," Graham says.

"And that's when I found the, the..." Jamie says, her words trailing off.

"The body," I say gently. I give the pair a moment, then I ask, "Did you see anything suspicious, anything at all that might be important to us?"

They exchange a look and shake their heads in unison. "Not really," Graham says.

"The footsteps," Jamie says. "I thought I heard footsteps upstairs."

"Was there someone up there?"

"I didn't see anyone, but I swear I heard them."

"Did you hear them, too?" I ask Graham.

"No. I didn't. I figured it was the old house settling."

We wrap up the interview and release them. They hurry to their truck quickly and drive away.

"Why do you look so interested in the creaking of an old house?" Tyler asks.

"Rylan thought she saw a woman on the porch earlier, and I didn't see anything."

"And you think it was a ghost. A ghost that Jamie Blake heard before discovering the body," Tyler interjects.

"Exactly."

"Maybe this one will talk to us."

"Can't hurt to try," I say.

TWENTY-ONE

RYLAN FLYNN

When my phone rings again a short time later, I want to ignore it. I want to stay buried in blankets and pillows, safe from the thing down the hall.

But it's Ford.

"Hey, Ry, you busy?"

I look around my crowded room, feeling a bit foolish for being in bed in the middle of the day. "No. Just hanging at home," I say, pushing blankets off.

"I, well, we, Tyler and I, wanted to ask you a favor."

"You want me to come talk to the ghost at the crime scene."

"You sure you're not psychic?"

"It was an obvious deduction. And no, I'm not psychic. If I was, I'd play the lotto." I chuckle at the bad joke. He chuckles, too, just a little.

"So you'll help us?"

"You know I'd do anything to help you, um, help your investigation."

"I really appreciate this." I hear Tyler say something in the background. "What time?"

"That's up to you. Tonight is good. The spirit will be

confused by all the activity at the house. She's most likely to want to be seen today."

"Just after dark? The techs should have the scene fully processed by then."

"I can be there. I'm not sure of Mickey's schedule, but I'll check with her."

"Thanks, Ry. As always, let's keep this between our little group."

"I understand." I do, but I can't help feeling a little hurt that he wants my involvement kept secret.

He grows silent for a few moments, so long, I wonder if he's still there. Finally, he asks, "Did you tell anyone about us going to see Miss Melanie the first time?"

The question catches me off guard. "I'm not sure, I think I might have told Dad, but Keaton already knew. Said you told him. Why?"

"Because Kaitlyn knew and I can't figure out how."

I do not want to talk about Kaitlyn. "I have no idea. It is a small town. Things get out." Plus, she's friends with Lindy.

"Maybe. Let's just keep this under our hats, okay."

"I already said I would." I'm growing irritated. "Look, if it's too much risk for you, I'll go with Mickey and just tell you what the ghost says."

"No way. We are coming, too."

He sounds excited, too excited. "You like this, don't you?"

"Like what?" He feigns innocence.

"Like talking to the ghosts. It's kind of addictive. I should know."

"Yeah, fine. I like it. Who wouldn't?"

"I'll see you tonight," I say, with a shake of my head and a warm feeling in my chest.

The yellow tape flutters in front of the house, bright streaks in the darkness. Mickey looks out the car window to the house.

"This place is rough," she says. "Some house flippers bought it?"

"That's what I was told."

"They have a big job ahead of them."

I turn off the engine and we sit in silence for a few moments.

"Do you see anything?" she whispers.

I look at the porch where I saw the ghost before. The porch is full of shadows, but none that look like a ghost. I'm not getting the tingle either.

"I don't see her or feel her," I whisper back, trying not to sound disappointed.

"You will," she says softly.

Headlights reflect off my rearview mirrors and I squint into the brightness. "They're here."

The slamming of our doors is loud in the quiet neighborhood. Most of the houses on the block are dark, only a few have lights on. The whole atmosphere is one of desolation. What once were nice homes filled with families are now empty, the dark windows like eyes watching us.

Ford and Tyler's boots are loud on the sidewalk as they walk toward us.

"Hey," Ford says. "You ready for this?" His voice is hushed, matching the quiet of the neighborhood.

I nod silently and turn up the walk.

Mickey puts the camera to her shoulder and begins filming. At the base of the steps to the porch, I turn and introduce the viewers to the scene. I doubt we'll ever use this footage, but I want it just in case.

"You guys ready?" I ask the camera with forced excitement. I am beginning to think this is not going to work. I still haven't felt a tingle of any kind. I don't want this to be a waste of time, and I truly want to find evidence to help solve the murder.

We make our way up the steps to the door.

I hesitate, my hand an inch from the handle. "Can I touch this?" I ask Ford. "I don't want to leave my prints at your crime scene."

"They've already processed everything," he says. "But just in case." He lifts the hem of his shirt and uses it to turn the knob.

The door swings open and he steps inside. "Ashby Police," he calls into the dark.

I exchange a look with Mickey, excited.

Tyler enters behind Ford and they take a quick look around with their flashlights. "All clear," Tyler says a minute later.

"Was that strictly necessary?" I ask as I step inside.

"Can't be too careful," Ford says. "You never know."

Mickey and I look around the room. "Seems like they just picked up and left without taking anything," she says.

There's a stuffed pink giraffe lying on the couch. "Did a kid live here?" I ask, pointing to the toy.

"A girl," Ford says. "Are you getting anything?" he asks hopefully.

I search my body for any signs, but I'm curiously devoid of tingles. I shake my head. "Sorry. Maybe she's not here right now."

He looks disappointed and then tries to hide it. "No worries."

"Maybe show me where her body was found."

"In the kitchen," Tyler says. I follow the men in that direction. Broken pieces of wood are scattered around the room. A sledgehammer lies among the debris.

"What happened in here?" Mickey asks.

"The house flippers were demoing the cabinets when they

found her." Ford points to a cabinet that is partly smashed in. "She was in there."

"In the cabinet?" I ask.

"Yep. Curled up."

Mickey gives an exaggerated shiver and films the cabinet, her light illuminating the dingy space.

"The poor thing." I look around the destroyed kitchen. "Hidden away like that. She must be scared." I still don't sense the ghost I saw earlier and it's starting to bother me. "Where is she?"

"Still nothing?" Ford asks with concern.

"Well, this was a long shot," Tyler points out, not unkindly.

"I'm sorry. As I've said, the ghosts do what they want."

"Maybe we should look upstairs?" Mickey offers.

We all file up the narrow steps, following the beam of Ford's flashlight. "The girl's room is this one," he says, opening a door. The bed only has sheets on it and the open closet is empty. The room has an eerie feeling about it, but no ghost.

We move on to the main bedroom. The moonlight shines in this window, illuminating the room.

"We think this is the woman we found," Ford says, showing me a wedding picture. I recognize the woman as the one I saw on the porch.

"That's her," I say, touching the picture. "I wonder where she is."

The floor downstairs creaks loudly. All four of us lift our heads, listening.

"What was that?" Mickey whispers.

Ford puts his hand on his gun, as does Tyler.

They sneak out the door.

The creak happens again, followed by a small crash.

"Dang it," a female voice exclaims.

Ford looks to me. "Is that her?"

I don't point out that only I could hear her talk if it was, I just shake my head.

Ford and Tyler creep down the stairs, guns drawn now. Mickey and I follow close behind.

At the bottom of the steps, Ford shouts, "Ashby Police, show yourself."

Something heavy hits the floor and a woman shouts, "Don't shoot."

TWENTY-TWO

RYLAN FLYNN

The woman stands among the broken shards in the kitchen, her hands in the air, the sledgehammer at her feet. The redhead squints into the beam of Ford's flashlight.

"Jamie Blake?" Tyler asks, lowering his gun.

"I'm sorry. Yes. I'm sorry." She shoves her hands even higher.

"Why are you here?" Ford asks, holstering his gun, but keeping the light on her face.

"Can I put my hands down?" she asks.

"Of course," Ford says. "Now explain to me why are you at a crime scene in the dark?"

"I needed my hammer," she says, frightened, pointing to the heavy tool nearby.

"Your hammer?" Tyler asks with disbelief.

"I know it's silly, but this hammer is special to me. Graham gave it to me for Christmas."

"A hammer as a Christmas present?" I ask.

Jamie jumps, startled by my presence. "Who's that?" she asks, blocking the flashlight with her hand.

I step around the men. The poor woman looks terrified. "I'm Rylan Flynn and that is my friend Mickey Ramirez."

Jamie's shoulders relax and she brushes her long red hair out of her face. "I don't understand. Why are all of you here?"

I look to Ford for help with that answer.

"Maybe it's better if you just take your hammer and leave," Ford says.

Footsteps creep across the ceiling from upstairs. Jamie lifts her eyes to the sound as do I. Everyone else seems oblivious.

"Do you hear that?" I ask the group.

Blank stares.

"Is there someone with you?" I ask Jamie.

"No. I came alone."

Then I realize it.

My back is tingling.

"What is it?" Mickey whispers, turning the camera back on.

I look into the lens. "There's footsteps in the hall upstairs. I think the ghost is here."

"Ghost?" Jamie asks.

"I'm a ghost investigator," I explain. "I saw her here, earlier today."

I expect Jamie to run away in fear. Instead, she picks up her hammer. "I knew it."

Motioning for them to follow me, I head back upstairs with Jamie close behind.

"Hello?" I question gently. "Is there someone up here?"

The sound of soft singing floats through the door of the little girl's room. I point to the door for the benefit of the camera. "She's in here," I say.

"I hear singing," Jamie says.

I turn, surprised. "Does anyone else hear it?"

More blank stares.

I just met this woman, is she playing a prank?

"What song is she singing?" I test her.

"That mockingbird one. You know, *hush little baby don't say a word, momma's gonna buy you a mockingbird.*"

Everyone looks to me for confirmation.

"She's right," I say in awe. "No one else hears it?"

Jamie seems uncomfortable. "I barely hear it, just a hum really. I recognize the tune."

The singing abruptly stops.

Jamie looks to me in question. "I think she heard us. Let's go in," I say.

I turn the handle and gently push the door in. It creaks slightly as it opens.

She's sitting on the bed, staring at the door.

The blonde woman I saw on the porch. The same one I saw in the picture of Lynette and Jacob.

She's dressed in jeans and a blue t-shirt that's stained with blood from where she was stabbed. She looks at me, her eyes full of questions.

I have my own questions.

"Do you see her?" I ask Jamie.

"I don't see anything." She sounds truly disappointed.

"Is she here?" Ford asks.

"She's sitting on the bed," I tell the group. "Are you Lynette?" I ask, although I'm sure she is.

"You can see me?"

"I can." I take a step into the room. Mickey is close behind with everyone crowding her.

"No one has been able to see me for years."

"I know. I'm different." I take another step closer, not wanting to startle her. "You're Lynette aren't you?"

"Yes." She looks over the group. "Who are all of you?" Her eyes land on Jamie. "You're the one that found me."

"She knows you're the one that found her," I tell Jamie.

"I am," Jamie says in the direction of the bed.

"Thank you," Lynette says. "I've waited for years."

I tell the group what she said. "Do you know what happened to you?" I ask gently.

"She didn't mean to do it." Lynette looks at her hands in her lap. "She really didn't."

"Who didn't mean it? Did a woman do this to you?" I motion to the bloody stab wounds in her chest.

"She was just mad, but that's not her."

I take another step and I'm directly in front of her. I crouch low, at eye level with her. "Lynette, you know who hurt you. Who was it?"

She suddenly lifts her head, her eyes wild. "Never mind. I will not tell you."

"We can help you. You just have to tell us what happened."

She jumps to her feet so suddenly, I flinch. "I will not hurt her. She was possessed. I know she was. That's not her." She storms across the room and reaches for a puppet on a shelf. Her hand goes right through it.

I stare at the puppet in terror.

I hate puppets.

She tries to pick it up again, but her hand goes through it. "Get out of my house," she shouts and swipes at the toy.

This time it flies across the room and crashes into the wall.

Everyone jumps, startled.

"Holy flip. Did you all see that?" I ask.

"We did," Mickey says. "And I got it on the camera." Her voice is shaking with excitement.

The ghost of Lynette is gone.

"Lynette?" I ask the room. "Lynette, come back."

Nothing.

"She's gone," I tell the camera and the group.

"Wow, that was cool," Jamie says, breathless.

Tyler and Ford exchange looks. "Guess we really are looking for a female killer," Ford says.

"Same as Melanie said," Tyler adds.

I look at the camera. "This is Rylan Flynn with *Beyond the Dead*. We had an interesting night tonight. Thanks for watching." I feel lame making my sign-off. I'll fix it in a voiceover later.

Jamie looks at the camera and back at me. "You making a documentary or something?"

"Kind of. We have a YouTube show where we investigate ghosts. Mickey films me talking to them and we post the footage."

Jamie seems impressed. "That's cool. I think I heard rumors that some local woman was a YouTube star."

"I'm not a star," I say, feeling foolish. "I'm just doing what I can for the spirits."

"So you can see them. Like really see them."

"She sure can," Mickey jumps in. "Ever since she was a little girl."

I look at the puppet on the floor. It is broken from where it smashed into the wall. Even so, it makes me shiver.

"Let's get out of here," I say, heading for the door.

We all file downstairs and out onto the front lawn before anyone speaks. Ford makes sure the front door is shut tight.

"Wish we had a key to lock this," Ford says. "Keep people out."

"Sorry about that again," Jamie says. "I really did want this hammer back." She lifts the red handle.

I wonder who Graham is and why a gift from him is so important.

She puts the hammer on her shoulder. "Wow. What a day. Found a murder victim then watched you talk to her ghost."

"And you heard her singing," I point out.

"Not really. I just kind of heard a song."

"You have some talent in this. That's super cool," I say, impressed.

Jamie shifts the hammer on her shoulder. "I don't think so. I'll leave that to you."

"You ready to go?" Mickey interrupts, shifting the camera from one hand to the other.

I look to Ford. "I guess so? Unless you needed anything else?"

"I think we're good." He looks at Tyler. It seems like Mickey is done for the night, but none of the rest of us want this to end.

"Do you do this a lot?" Jamie asks.

"Talk to ghosts?"

"Consult for the police?"

"She's not really a consultant," Ford says stiffly. "And on that point. We were never here. You were never here." He stands tall, imposing.

"Of course not," Jamie says with a wink. The wink makes me like her even more.

Mickey pulls on my shirt sleeve. "Let's go. Marco is waiting."

I say my goodbyes and allow myself to be led to the car.

We drive in silence for a few minutes. We don't rock out to music like we usually would. Somehow, it doesn't seem like music time.

When I turn onto Mickey's block, I finally ask.

"Are you okay?"

She doesn't look away from the window. "Of course."

"You don't seem okay."

"Well, I am. Just drop it."

"Want me to come by tomorrow and go over tonight's footage?" I venture.

"We can't use it anyway. Not until the murder investigation is long over. And, even then, we probably shouldn't be at an active crime scene. We're going to get in trouble. What if that woman presses charges on us for trespassing?" I park in her driveway and she instantly opens her door.

"She wouldn't do that," I say.

"You'd know."

"Seriously, Mickey. What's wrong?" I ask, as she reaches into the backseat for her camera.

She sighs heavily, the camera in her lap. "Nothing. I mean it. I'm just tired."

I don't believe her, but I let it slide. She'll tell me if she wants to.

"Have a good night," I say lamely.

She stares at me a moment, then seems to grow angry again. She climbs out of the car without another word, slamming the door behind her.

I drive home alone.

I should be excited and keyed up after such an interesting encounter.

I'm not.

TWENTY-THREE

BESS

Earlier

I'm so shocked by the man's voice below me I stop pounding on the trap door.

"Who's there?" I shout down the stairs.

A figure fills the space on the bottom step. A man. But not the man who brought me here. This is someone I don't recognize.

"You really need to stay calm, Bess," he says.

Missy squeals, "Daddy, you came," and joins him. Her pale round face looks up the steps. "She's not behaving, Daddy. You should get another one."

"She'll settle in soon enough."

"What's going on? Where's the other man?"

How did you get in here? Is there another way out?

"Bess, come down and I'll explain it all."

He's not too much older than me and has kindly eyes. I'm so scared I cling to that scrap of kindness and descend to him.

"You'll tell me what's going on? Why was I brought here?"

He motions for me to sit on the couch. I sink onto the flat

cushions and look up to the man. Missy flounces onto the couch next to me. I resist the urge to scoot away from her.

"Turn that off," the man tells her and she clicks the cartoons away. "You've met my daughter, Missy, obviously. Sorry I wasn't here to greet you when you arrived."

"That's okay." I can't believe I'm forgiving him when I'm held here against my will. I have some faint idea that he might help me escape if I stay on his good side.

"She showed you your room?"

I nod.

"She didn't like it," Missy says. "I told you to get a new blanket."

He shoots his daughter a quieting look. "I'm Jacob. And this is our home."

I look again for another door, for a way he got in. I still see concrete walls painted a pale shade of yellow that has begun peeling.

"How did you get in?"

Missy laughs. "They always ask that."

Confused, I look to the little girl, afraid of her cryptic references to others. "Are there other people down here?" I ask hopefully.

"Just you and Missy."

"Please tell me what's going on. I came here with a different man. Where is he?"

"He did what he was supposed to. Now it's just us," Jacob says.

"What does that mean?"

Missy bounces on the couch cushions. "Tell her about Mommy. Tell her."

"This all started a few years ago when Missy and I moved in here."

"Where's her mother?" I demand, looking around the room as if her mother will suddenly appear.

"She's dead," Missy shouts, bouncing again. She seems to enjoy the news.

I look to Jacob for confirmation. He nods sadly. "Missy's mother died, shortly before we came here." He quiets Missy with another look. She practically quivers with excitement.

"Tell her how she died."

Jacob's face fills with sadness again and a touch of something else. Fear?

"She died. Let's just leave it at that."

Missy's mood switches in an instant. "Tell her," she demands.

Now the fear is evident in her father's expression.

"She doesn't need to know that part."

"I stabbed her," Missy says. "She wouldn't let me stay up to play with my puppet, so I stabbed her."

I look to Jacob for confirmation. He looks down, hiding his expression, but his whole demeanor gives him away.

She's telling the truth.

TWENTY-FOUR

RYLAN FLYNN

As I wait in my kitchen for coffee to brew, I send a text to Mickey.

Are you free to help Sarah tonight?

We already discussed it and tonight was the agreed-on time, but I don't know what else to use as an excuse to contact her. I desperately want to confirm we are okay, want this itch of something wrong between us to go away.

By the time the coffee finishes brewing, I still haven't gotten a reply.

Strictly speaking, I could help Sarah to cross over without Mickey and the camera, but I don't want to. She's always been there and I need her support.

I lean against the crowded counter and drink my coffee while I wait for her reply.

My phone finally chirps. One word.

Yep.

That's not good. When Mickey says yep instead of yes, I know she's annoyed.

"What did I do?" I ask the packed kitchen.

I think back to last night and all that was said. I can't remember anything that happened that would set her off.

I drink the last swallow of my coffee and set the cup next to numerous others on the counter.

The sink has several plates and forks in it as well as a bowl with dried cereal on the rim. I stare at the mess, then turn slowly to inspect the kitchen. I'm fully aware that my hoarding has taken over the house. I've seen the shows, I know what I am.

But I've prided myself that I'm not one of "those hoarders." I'm not dirty. I just like to keep things.

My trash is overflowing and there are empty containers on the floor.

"Holy flip, how did this mess get here?" I ask the piles.

With sudden vigor, I shove the trash in the bag and haul the bag out to the dumpster. I fill it again with all the empties on the floor. I then fill the sink with suds and wash every dirty dish I see.

An hour later, I'm hot and my hair is plastered to my forehead.

And I feel good. Real good.

My kitchen is still full of boxes and a few pieces of furniture I rescued, but the counters are clear and the sink is empty.

I even cleaned out the fridge, which was a whole adventure of its own.

Feeling proud of myself, and riding the high, I finally try Candy again.

She answers on the first ring.

"Candy, it's Rylan from the other night."

"Of course, Rylan, I remember. Is everything okay? I didn't expect to hear from you guys. Not after, you know..."

"Everything's good, I just have to ask a favor. I talked to the ghost, Sarah, again later that night. And I'm fairly certain she was murdered."

A sharp intake of breath. "Murdered?"

"By her Uncle Ralph. I did a little digging and it seems he wanted the property and killed Sarah's parents, and then her, so he could inherit."

"You're talking about Ralph Carrillo? He's my husband's great-grandpa. Antonio inherited this house in a direct line from him."

A deep silence follows as she realizes her husband's ancestor was a murderer. "How sure are you about this?" she says in a low voice. I wonder if Antonio is close by and can overhear.

"I'm fairly certain. I heard it straight from Sarah."

"She said she was murdered?" she whispers.

"Not directly, but it was the only conclusion that could be drawn."

"How?"

"I'm thinking she and her parents were poisoned."

"Antonio is not going to like this," she says in the same low voice. "Do we have to tell him?"

I hear the unspoken implication. An angry Antonio is bad for Candy. The last thing I want to do is make trouble for her.

I shake my charm bracelet, thinking. "I mean, no. There's no reason we have to tell him."

"Thank you, thank you," she gushes. "Now what do you need from me?"

"What I want to do is a bit unusual, even for us. Sarah is looking for her mother, Diana, and has chosen you for her mother here still on earth."

"Right..." she says hesitantly.

"I have a friend that might be able to help us reach Diana. If we can bring Diana here, Dad and I can help Sarah cross over."

"You want to bring a spirit back from the beyond?"

"That's kind of the plan." Now that she's said it out loud it sounds a bit ludicrous. "I don't want to just send Sarah over by herself."

"I can see that. And you want to do this here?"

"Will Antonio be okay with that?"

"Um, I don't think so."

"We could do it in the cemetery near her gravesite. Would that work better?"

"Yes." She's so relieved that I find myself worrying again about the state of her marriage. "Just tell me when and I'll be there."

"I'll call you back after I get everyone else set up."

"Okay. And, Rylan, thank you for including me. I know it's silly, but I feel responsible for her now that I know she's the one that's been haunting me. Last night, she sat on the settee with me for a long time and I could almost imagine her there."

"She was there," I say gently. "She needs you."

"It's nice to be needed."

The cryptic comment makes me sad. "Yes it is," I agree. "I'll text you the time and see you tonight."

The next call I make is to Lorraine, also known as the White Witch. I met her a few months ago at a paranormal fair and she helped me out recently. I hope she won't mind me asking for help again.

And I hope what I need her for is in the realm of her abilities.

I've helped souls cross over, but I have never called one from the other side. Maybe together we can pull this off.

Lorraine seems pleased to hear from me again.

"Rylan, what a surprise."

I want to tease, isn't she a psychic and already knew I was going to call, but I hate when people make that joke to me and won't stoop to that level. Still, I'm nervous.

I dive right in.

"I need to ask for your help with a situation."

"You have my attention. What can I do for you?"

I tell her all about Sarah, about my plan.

"I know it's a bit far out there," I say, feeling foolish.

"Not too far out there. I've been asked to reach those on the other side lots of times. I've just never helped a soul cross over on top of that. It sounds most intriguing."

"Does that mean you'll help?"

"I'm in."

Dad is just as easy to convince to help. He readily agrees to the time and place.

I have one more person I want to talk to before we do the séance.

I don't like feeling that Mickey is upset with me. I need all my energy and attention to be on Sarah tonight, I can't let this dust-up with Mickey weigh on me. I've texted her as the pieces of tonight have fallen into place, but besides the "yep" I got this morning, she's been curiously silent.

I finally can't take it anymore and I drive to her house.

I normally would just walk in, but I knock this time.

Waiting on the porch, I shuffle my feet, going over last night in my head again.

The door opens and her dark curly hair and anger-pinched face fills the gap. She doesn't invite me in.

"You should take the hint that I don't want to talk to you."

"I got the hint, that's why I'm here. Mickey, what's wrong?"

She squints her eyes. "Why don't you go ask Jamie?"

"Jamie who? Oh wait, that woman from last night? I'm totally confused."

"You weren't confused about her last night. You were practically gushing over how she could hear that ghost."

I can hardly believe it. Mickey's jealous.

"I don't care about that."

"You sure seemed to care last night." She crosses her arms and leans against the door jamb.

"Okay, yes, I was excited that someone other than me could hear the ghost, but I don't understand why that makes you mad."

"I'm not mad." She lifts her chin.

"You sound mad."

"I'm, I'm... I don't know what I am. I just didn't like the way you were acting." She looks at my shoes.

"I wasn't acting any way. I was just keyed up after the encounter, the way I always am."

"Why do you do the show with me?" she asks suddenly.

I stare at her, feel my mouth fall open. "Why do you think?"

"You tell me."

"You're my best friend and my business partner. In all the world, there is no one I trust more."

"But I can't see the ghosts."

There it is.

"But you do everything else. There is no show without you."

"You could find another camera person," she tries. I sense the break in her armor.

"Not one as good as you. Plus you do all the editing and the marketing and the uploading to the internet. I don't know any of that stuff."

She smiles.

"Yeah, you basically walk around and talk and I do the rest."

"Exactly. Plus, you're the best best friend anyone could ask for."

She opens the door wide to let me in. "Let's make a plan for tonight. Also, I need you to do some voiceovers."

"See, no show without you in charge of it."

"Oh, just shut up," she teases.

I feel tension leaving my body. We're going to be fine.

TWENTY-FIVE

FORD PIERCE

I look at the file folders on my desk with disgust. Three major cases open right now. How is that possible in a small town like Ashby?

I flip through each, turning over the details in my mind. Melanie Shaw was stabbed in the back. She said by a woman. Can I trust that fact, seeing as it came from a ghost? A fact that has been verified is that she spent her last known night with her sister at the Juke Joint. Her sister left her there to finish her drink. The bartender says a man joined Melanie and they eventually left together.

No video from the bar.

No other corroborating accounts, and the bartender was vague in his description. White man, possibly in his thirties with brownish hair, maybe.

That's all I have to go on. A maybe and a comment from a ghost.

I shut the folder and move on to the next one.

The body found yesterday. No matching missing person's reports. Marrero called late in the day yesterday and confirmed she was stabbed in the chest. Twice. As with Melanie, Lynette said a woman was responsible.

Is there a woman out there killing other women and leaving their bodies on abandoned properties? How does that tie in with Melanie last being seen with a man at the bar?

Another dead end, so I close that folder and lay it on top of the other one.

The last folder, I open with dread.

Bess Freeman.

Where in the world is she?

Is she even still alive?

I have to hope. I remember Bess from when Kaitlyn and I were dating, although she didn't make much of an impression. She was the bookish, quiet partner to Kaitlyn's more outgoing personality. Their team worked well and they grew their clothing business to a sizable online store.

I look at Bess's picture in the file. A dimple peeks out from her cheek, her smile is tentative. Her eyes are kind. I touch the picture. "Bess, where are you?" I whisper.

I read through Rylan's statement of the man she saw Bess leave with. On the surface, it is similar to the description given for Melanie's case.

On the surface, it's a description of half the men in Ashby.

I read through the rest of the file. Interviews with Bess's friends and family. Her co-workers. No one had a motive to hurt her.

The only motive, as flimsy as it is, is the life insurance policy Kaitlyn has on Bess. To be fair, Bess has one on Kaitlyn as well. Standard practice for business partners.

I mull that angle over.

Money, love, revenge. The classic motives for murder.

Kaitlyn had a monetary motive to want Bess gone.

She loved Bess. But most people are murdered by someone they know, often someone they once loved or still love.

Revenge. Is there something in their relationship that we don't know? Could Kaitlyn want Bess gone for some business disagreement?

Kaitlyn was at the bottom of my list of favorite people for several months after we broke up, but, even after seeing her at her very worst, I cannot make my mind think she has anything to do with Bess's disappearance.

Am I being naïve?

Am I grasping at straws?

This is a dangerous road to go down. I look at the picture of Bess's shy smile and decide I must at least look into all the angles of what happened to her. I owe it to Bess.

Tyler suddenly breezes into our office, talking on the phone. "Okay, got it. Thanks for the info," he says, then hangs up.

"What's up?" I ask when he sits in his chair.

"We got the property search info back on that flip house. Before the bank took it back, it was owned by a Jacob and Lynette Reed. I was just talking to the bank and they said that after years of making consistent payments, they suddenly quit paying their mortgage. The bank had to foreclose after they couldn't reach the Reeds."

"And Jamie Blake bought it from the bank. Okay. So when did they stop making payments?"

"Four years ago."

"Which matches with the estimated window for time of death that Marrero gave. So Jacob kills his wife, stashes her body in a cabinet, and takes off with the little girl."

"Looks like it."

"So we need to find him." I'm excited to have a direction.

"There's only one problem," Tyler says.

"What's that?"

"Rylan told us Lynette said she was killed by a woman."

"I was thinking about that earlier," I say. "How much stock can we put in what a ghost tells us?"

"You think Rylan made it up?"

"No. But maybe Lynette did. We know nothing about her. Maybe she's confused. Maybe she's making it up. Rylan said half the time they don't even know they're dead."

Tyler leans back in his chair. "You think Lynette lied? I guess, maybe."

"We need to follow the facts first. Let's see what we can find out about this Jacob. What was the last name?"

"Reed."

"Didn't Melanie mention someone with the name Reed?" I ask, sitting up straighter.

Tyler gives me a blank look.

I open a different folder on my desk, one where I've been keeping notes from our encounters with Rylan.

"When Miss Melanie got upset, she called for someone called Reed."

"Reed is a popular name in town. I knew a few of them in high school."

"Could be. Still, kind of a strange coincidence."

"I thought you didn't believe in coincidences," Tyler teases.

"Exactly."

"Miss Melanie said she was murdered by a woman, too," Tyler points out. "Do you think they're both lying?"

"That would be a coincidence."

Tyler rubs at his face with both hands. "Okay, where do you want to start with this?"

Bess's picture is still looking at me. "I think we need to work on Bess. We might still be able to save her. Melanie and Lynette have been dead a long time. They can wait a little while longer."

"So what do you want to do there? Have we heard back from tech on her computer yet?"

"Not yet. I'll check with them and see if they can expedite it." I chew on my lower lip, wondering if I should mention Kaitlyn. I owe it to Bess to go down every road. "I want to float something by you."

Tyler looks up, concerned by my change in tone.

"I've been thinking about who would have a motive to hurt Bess, to get rid of her. Maybe we're missing the obvious."

He sits forward. "Okay. What did you come up with?"

I look at the wall behind him. Am I really going to say this out loud?

"Hello, Earth to Ford." Tyler waves his hand in front of my face.

"I don't want to say this, but what if Kaitlyn had something to do with it? Maybe she paid someone to make Bess go away." The words sound ridiculous to my ears.

"Kaitlyn?" He mulls it over. "She does have that insurance policy on Bess. Maybe there was some beef down at the clothing company that we haven't uncovered yet."

"So I'm not crazy for thinking this?"

"Not crazy, but this could really backfire on you, if she finds out we're even entertaining the thought she did this."

"And where is the body?" I add. "She'd need a body for insurance."

"That's true. It's not a strong case. But it's something to look into."

"Can you go back down to their business and talk to all the employees again? Maybe one of them knows about some issue between Kaitlyn and Bess that we missed the first time."

"I can do that," Tyler stands. "I'll go now. You check in with tech on Bess's computer."

"One of us needs to call Marrero and give him the name of the body he's working on. As far as he's concerned, she's still a Jane Doe. He'll need to confirm she's Lynette Reed."

"Sounds like a good job for you once you're done with tech," Tyler says, then hurries out the door.

Better Marrero than Kaitlyn finding out I'm looking into her.

———

It only takes a short time to talk to the techs. Short because they are not done with Bess's computer yet. I console myself with no news being good news and return to our office to call Marrero. I tell him we are fairly certain the Jane Doe is Lynette Reed. He grumbles in response, but agrees to do a dental record confirmation.

With all that done, I sit and flip through the files again, waiting on Tyler to return. I wonder how things are going over at the clothing business. I hate to sit out on the re-questioning, but I don't think it will lead anywhere anyway.

There's nothing I can do for Bess right now, so I turn my attention to Lynette Reed.

Reed.

Yes, it is a common name in the town, but there must be some connection. It can't be coincidence that the name would come up in two different investigations.

On a hunch, I check the employee records for the church where Melanie Shaw was working as a daycare worker. Unity Church. They list a Robert Reed as janitor.

"Well, hello Robert Reed," I say to my computer monitor. "Think we need to chat."

———

Unity Church on Highway 7 is a large, newly built building. Besides the spire on the front, it looks more like a pole barn than a church. It's a far cry from the bricks and broken stained glass in the church where we saw Melanie.

"Smells better than the other church," Tyler says as we walk in. A hint of vanilla and cinnamon fills the front lobby. Everything is clean and inviting. I absently look through pamphlets set up on a table as we wait.

Robert Reed greets us a few moments later. "Detectives, sorry to keep you waiting," he says with a question in his eyes. "Thank you for meeting us on such short notice," I say. "I'm Ford Pierce and this is Tyler Spencer." He leads us to some benches, but doesn't sit himself.

I sit casually, open, hoping to put the janitor at ease. He shuffles his feet, my body language not helping calm him. "This will just take a few minutes," I assure him.

"Good, good. Whatever you need." Reed finally sits. "You said this was about Melanie Shaw?"

"We understand she was also employed here," Tyler says. "In the daycare."

"Yes, she was. She was wonderful with the kids. We missed her greatly when she disappeared."

"How long did she work here?" Tyler asks.

"Let me see..." Reed leans back in his chair, his tension lessening. "I'd say about two years. Yeah, that seems right. Two years."

I search his face for any resemblance to the man in the video of Bess. Looking at him straight on, he doesn't seem familiar. More accurately, he looks like most white men in town. He could be anyone. This might be a wild goose chase.

"How well did you know Melanie?" Tyler asks. "Did you have just a working relationship?"

Reed shifts in his seat at the sudden question. "What do you mean?" he asks, his defenses up now.

"I think you know what I mean," Tyler pushes.

Reed looks around the lobby. "I, we... We were friends," he stammers, obviously not telling the whole truth.

"Did you see her outside of here?" I ask. "Neither of you were married, it isn't a sin to date, is it?"

"We didn't date." He looks up, suddenly. "Look, yes, we saw each other outside of church, but we were just close friends. We didn't date. It wasn't romantic." Reed leans toward us. "I didn't have anything to do with her disappearance. I especially didn't hurt her and leave her body in that abandoned lot. I cared for her."

"Caring for her and hurting her aren't mutually exclusive," Tyler says.

"I did not hurt her," he states emphatically.

"What about Bess Freeman?" I ask. "Did you know her?"

Reed sighs heavily. "I saw on the news that she is missing, too."

"She disappeared from The Lock Up several nights ago. We have a video of the suspect but it's hard to make out," I say.

"That's promising." I search his face, his body language. He's nervous about something.

"The man in the video looks a lot like you," I state. Tyler looks at me in surprise then looks back at Reed. I can tell by his face that he now sees the resemblance too.

"It can't be me," he says desperately.

"Where were you Friday night, late?" I ask.

"I was home."

"Can anyone corroborate that?"

He hangs his head. "No. I was alone."

"Do you believe in ghosts?" Tyler interjects.

Reed raises his head. "That's an interesting question. One I am surprised would come up in a murder investigation. Does this have anything to do with that ghost hunter woman? I heard a rumor she was working with the police."

"You know about Rylan Flynn?" I ask.

"I know about what she does with ghosts. I'm not convinced the whole thing is real."

"What if we told you we talked to the ghost of Melanie Shaw?" Tyler plunges in.

"I'd say prove it."

I shift in my seat. This isn't going the way I need it to. I change tactics. "Mr. Reed, does the name Jacob Reed mean anything to you?"

He blanches white. "Why?"

"Does it?"

"He was my brother."

"Was?" Tyler asks.

"He and his family left town a few years back. I haven't heard from him since. We're not exactly family now I'd say."

"Do you know where he went?"

"He didn't tell me. He just said they were tired of the winters here and wanted to go somewhere warmer. Said he'd let me know when they got settled. I never heard from him again."

"You didn't think that was strange?" I ask.

"I did. But you have to understand. Jacob was always the paranoid type. He got into that prepper stuff. You know, self-sustained farms and such. He was sure the world was going to collapse and his dream was to own a farm where he could raise his own food. Live off the grid kind of stuff."

"You don't know where he went?" I ask.

"I figure he went off-grid like he always dreamed. If he doesn't want to talk to me, I don't need to talk to him," he says with a note of pain.

"You said he left with his family. Would that be a little girl and his wife?" I ask.

"Yes." Reed begins to look concerned. "What is this about?"

"You haven't seen Jacob or Lynette in how long?" I ask.

"Four years, I think. Look, Detectives, I'm getting worried here. What's going on? Did you find Jacob? Has something happened?"

"Was Jacob ever a violent man?" Tyler asks. "Did he and Lynette have troubles in their marriage?"

"Not that I know of." Reed looks from my face to Tyler's. "What's happened?"

"I'm sorry, but we believe the remains of Lynette Reed were found yesterday."

He sinks into his chair. "What do you mean remains? She and Jacob are on some farm somewhere warm."

"No. She's dead. Has been dead a long time. Looks like your brother killed her and then took off."

"That's not possible," he breathes. "Jacob wouldn't hurt anyone."

"She was found in their abandoned house," I say.

"His house? I thought he sold that."

"The bank took it. And recently sold it to new owners."

Reed looks blankly to the far wall of the lobby. "Jacob killed Lynette? There's no way."

"Do you have any idea where he may be now?" Tyler asks.

"None. Like I said, I haven't heard from him since he and Lynette left town. Oh no. She never left. This is all too much." He looks back to the wall of the lobby. "Wait, what about Missy?"

TWENTY-SIX

BESS

Earlier

Missy stabbed her mother? That can't be true. She must be playing some trick on me.

"They never believe me," Missy pouts. "Make her believe, Daddy."

"Missy needs a new mom," Jacob says instead. "And you, Bess, have been chosen to be that mom."

"I don't know anything about being a mom," I protest. "I just want to go home."

"I told you this is home!" Missy screams. "Make her understand."

Jacob crouches before me so his eyes are on a level with mine. He stares intently. "You must not upset her. That is rule number one here."

I look away from his intense gaze.

"Do you understand?" he asks.

"I understand," I mutter. "Sorry, Missy. Yes, this is home. A lovely home."

Missy glows at her victory.

"Where did you come from?" I ask Jacob. "Is there another room I haven't seen?"

He looks upset at my questions. "I think it's time you made her some lunch."

Is it lunch time? What time is it? The last moment I remember, before waking up at the bottom of the stairs, was late at night. Could hours have passed so quickly?

My grumbling stomach tells me it doesn't matter. Whichever time of day it is, it's time to eat.

I glance at Missy, then at Jacob. "What would you like for lunch, Missy?" I ask as sweetly as I can.

"Ravioli," Missy says excitedly.

I look over my shoulder at the well-stocked shelves. "There are cans of ravioli there. In fact, everything you should ever need is there," Jacob says.

I don't like the sound of that.

I walk to the shelves and find the stack of ravioli cans. "Would you like me to make enough for three?" I ask.

But, when I turn around, Jacob is gone.

TWENTY-SEVEN

RYLAN FLYNN

"I hope the church board doesn't find out about this," Dad says as he joins Mickey and me in the church parking lot. "They look the other way concerning our other adventures, but one performed on church grounds? That might be an issue."

I point to the camera in Mickey's hand. "You do know we are filming this for our show. Someone is bound to find out."

Dad freezes for a moment. "Oh yeah. That."

I'm torn. I need the footage, but I don't want to get Dad into trouble either.

"Of course, I doubt many on the church board watch the show. If they do, they probably wouldn't admit it." He shrugs. "And, besides, Sarah's soul is more important than wagging tongues."

I relax. I really need this footage. We have to have something to post for the show. Mickey and I have bills to pay.

A car pulls in and parks next to my Caddy. "That must be Lorraine, the White Witch. Wait until you meet her, she's a gem."

I'm not sure what to expect when the car door opens. I've

seen her dressed in flowing robes as well as jeans and a button-up flannel. Which Lorraine will show up tonight?

A long skirt slides out the open door, spilling onto the gravel. I anxiously wait to see the rest of the outfit.

Lorraine didn't disappoint. She's dressed in a simple, yet flowing, white dress with wide sleeves that swirl around her when she moves her arms. Her long dark hair hangs loose, blowing softly in the night breeze. Bracelets jangle on both wrists.

She dressed for the part.

I look down at my skinny jeans, black long-sleeve t-shirt and black Converse sneakers. Maybe I should update my wardrobe. I try to picture myself in a dress like Lorraine's and almost laugh out loud. She makes it look amazing and mysterious. I get the feeling I'd look like I was wearing a costume.

She joins our little group with a flourish. I introduce her to Mickey and Dad and they all exchange pleasantries.

"Thank you for coming," I tell her. "I don't know if this will work, but I wanted to have all the help I can get."

"Is she here?" Lorraine looks over the cemetery.

"This cemetery always fills me with tingles, so something is here. Not sure if it's Sarah or someone else."

"Hello," a voice says in the dark. Dad spins around, startled.

It's not Sarah. It's Candy.

She steps tentatively into our group, eyeing Lorraine with open interest. Lorraine introduces herself. Candy takes the offered hand gingerly.

"You ready for this?" I ask her.

"I hope so. Just tell me what to do."

"First, let's go over to Sarah's headstone. I think that's the best place to try."

We all walk through the dark. The further we get from the parking area, the more shadows engulf us. We lower our voices when we arrive at the headstone with the angel sitting on top.

"Sarah Carrillo," Candy reads. "So strange that's been here with our name on it all this time," she says vaguely.

"Most everyone in town has a relative or two in here," Dad says.

Candy looks up, makes a brave face. "I guess so. Not everyone is being haunted, though."

"You'd be surprised," Mickey says. "We get a lot of requests."

"You do?" Lorraine asks, genuinely interested.

"More than you'd think," Mickey replies.

Dad rubs his hands up and down his arms. "Let's get started," he says, looking to me for guidance.

Everyone else is looking at me, too. Mickey has her camera on. "I don't feel anything," I say with regret. "A little tingle, but nothing definite."

I step away from the group and put my hand on the headstone. "Sarah, are you here?" I ask to the sky.

Lorraine is suddenly by my side, her hand on mine. "Sarah, it's okay. You can join us."

A tingle swims in my belly as a white nightgown forms before me.

"She's here," I whisper. "Hello, Sarah. Nice to see you again."

"Have you found my mommy?" she asks, her pale face pinched. "I want her." Sarah looks past me at Candy. She walks through the headstone and joins her. "Mommy?"

"She's reaching for you," I tell Candy. "Directly in front of you."

"Hello, Sarah," Candy says tentatively.

"Let's see if we can call Diane, her mother," I say to the camera, then look to Lorraine. "What do we do?"

She reaches for my hand, then for Dad's. Candy joins us and we make a circle.

Dad begins to pray. Lorraine begins to chant.

"What are you doing?" Sarah asks from the center of the circle.

"We're trying to find your mommy," I tell her. "I need you to think really hard, okay. Think about your mom, picture her in your mind. Can you do that?"

Sarah scrunches her eyes tight and thinks hard.

"She's doing it," I say to the group.

"Please, Lord, guide this soul back to you. Take her into your arms and give her the peace only you can give," Dad is praying.

"Diane, come for your daughter, guide her home with you. Take her to her eternal resting place," Lorraine chants into the sky.

Candy watches in rapt attention, her mouth open slightly. She squeezes my hand hard. I squeeze back in encouragement.

The bugs that had been singing fall silent. All you can hear is the chanting and praying. I wonder for the hundredth time if this will work. I've called spirits to me from this side, but never from beyond.

I wonder absently if Bess would come if I called to her, but push that away. I need to focus on Diane.

The slight night breeze picks up a few notches, the wind lifting our hair. Lorraine's blows out behind her as she turns her face to the moon and chants for Diane.

"I'm scared," Sarah says. "What's happening?"

"You're going home," I tell her gently.

Behind her headstone, a light begins to grow. A small ball at first, then a larger glow.

"It's working," I say, excited.

Dad prays louder. Lorraine leans her head back, calling to the stars.

"Diane, come to us, come to us. Come for your daughter."

The light grows big and Sarah cowers behind me. In the middle of the light, a figure forms.

"I think she's coming," I whisper. "I see someone in the light."

Is it Diane? I suddenly realize the powers we are playing with. I think of the thing in Keaton's room. Not all spirits are kindly. I want to stop this, but it's too late. I shake with fear at the approaching figure.

"I feel something coming," Dad says, "Stay together now."

Out of the corner of my eye, I see the camera dip from Mickey's shoulder as she cowers, no doubt sensing the pulses of energy around us from the glowing light. Sarah tries to hide behind my legs.

Beyond the figure, I see a dark shadow and I can't stop staring at it. Lorraine must have seen it too because she lets out a wail.

"Sarah?" A woman's voice calls from the glowing circle. "My dear."

I almost collapse with relief.

Sarah peeks from behind my legs. "Mommy?"

The figure grows, takes the form of a woman. She stands in the light, reaching. The shadow behind her reaches too. I try to focus on Diane. "Come to me, Sarah. Let's go home."

Sarah looks to Candy, then to her mother. "I need to go now," she says to Candy.

"You go, Sarah," Candy says.

"Thank you for being my mommy while my real mommy was gone."

I repeat the words, my voice catching.

"My pleasure," Candy says, her own voice thick with emotion.

"Lord, take this soul into your arms, into your eternal home," Dad prays.

Diane's hand is still reaching from the light. The shadow close behind her.

"Hurry, Sarah," I urge.

Sarah puts her tiny hand in her mother's and steps forward.

"Thank you for taking care of my daughter," Diane says to me. "Thank you, all of you."

My chest is tight and I feel my eyes stinging with both fear and emotion. "We are happy to do it," I manage to say. "Good-bye, Sarah."

Sarah waves and steps further into the light.

As suddenly as the light appeared, it is gone. A tendril of shadow extends from the empty space a moment, then fades away.

"She's gone," I say, letting out a huge sigh of relief. I don't tell them about the shadow.

"Phew, that was amazing," Dad says. "She really passed over, didn't she?" He's buzzing with excitement.

Lorraine is curiously quiet, looking at the ground.

"You okay?" I ask her. "That was intense."

Lorraine looks up. "That really happened?" she asks, full of wonder.

"Yes, it did."

"I... I've never done anything like that. Wow. I didn't actually think this would work when you asked me to help." She gives me a curious look.

"Did you see her?" I ask.

She nods. "A little. It was more like I could feel her." She looks like she wants to say more, but shrugs it off. "Wow. That's all I can say."

"I'm glad you were here. We couldn't have done it without you."

"Candy?!" A male voice calls from Candy's porch next door, making us all jump.

Candy wipes her eyes quickly. "Oh, that's Antonio. I've got to get back. I didn't tell him what we were doing. He wouldn't understand."

Antonio sees us congregated in the cemetery and starts down the porch stairs.

Candy gives me a quick hug, whispers, "thank you" in my ear, and hurries out of the cemetery.

"What in the world are you doing out here?" Antonio demands. "Is that those ghost hunter frauds?" He stares hard across his yard. I stare back, defiant.

"Let's just go back inside," she says and leads him away. "We were just talking."

"Leave my wife alone, you freaks," he shouts then turns away.

Candy stops and stares at him. "Do not talk to my friends like that."

I'm impressed she stood up to him.

"Nice guy," Lorraine says.

"Yeah. He's not too fond of us." I look to Mickey. She gives me a thumbs up. She got the whole encounter with Antonio on camera.

"Forget him," Dad says. "We did great work here tonight."

The breeze has died back down and the night bugs are singing again.

Mickey turns off the camera. "Wow, that was intense," she says. "Diane really came?"

"She did. We did it. All of us, together. And Sarah is home," I say.

"Talking of home, it's getting late," Dad says. "That was really something, though." He kisses me on the cheek. "Never a dull moment with this one," he tells Lorraine.

She gives a weak smile. "I see that. It was nice to meet you all," she adds as she makes her way to her car. "I'd better get going, too. I have an hour drive."

I hurry across the cemetery to catch her. "Thanks for your help. Truly."

"Call me anytime," she says and squeezes my hand. "I'm so impressed with what you do."

I don't know how to respond. "You, too," I say lamely.

Mickey stands next to me as Dad and Lorraine drive away.

"Want to listen to Panic! At the Disco?" she asks.

"Do I ever." In the car, Mickey pulls up our favorite song on her phone and we blast out to the music all the way home.

I feel good. So good.

TWENTY-EIGHT

RYLAN FLYNN

When I hear pounding, I think it is the thing in Keaton's room as usual.

This time it's calling my name.

"Rylan Flynn, I know you're in there."

I sit up in bed and check the time. It's just past two a.m.

"What in the world?" I grumble, sliding across the piles of blankets on my bed.

More knocking. It's on the front door.

"I'm not leaving here until you come out and talk to me."

It's a man's voice, vaguely familiar, but I can't place it.

He continues to bellow as I make my way through the paths in my house.

"You caused this," he shouts, banging again on my front door.

I check the peep hole and see an eye looking back at me.

I jump back.

"Who's there?"

"You open this door." More banging.

"Go away or I'm calling the police."

"You call all the police you want. You put Candy up to this. You will now face the consequences."

Candy? Oh no, this must be Antonio.

I flip on the porch light, then slide the door chain into the lock and crack the door open. "I have no idea what you are talking about," I say through the crack.

He runs both hands through his hair, making it stick up wildly.

"She kicked me out," he says miserably.

A rush of pride in Candy flushes through me. From what I've seen of Antonio, Candy deserves better.

"I'm sorry to hear that," I lie. "But how is that my fault?"

"You went poking into things that were none of your business."

"If you're talking about Sarah, she is my business."

"Candy said you are claiming my great-grandpa murdered some little girl and her parents to get our house. That I have a murderer in my family."

"I'm sorry if that upsets you, but it's true."

"Says a ghost. If that ghost is even real. You just made up lies to ruin my life."

"I only listened to Sarah and she told me the truth."

"She isn't real." He advances suddenly to the crack in the door and I pull back.

"You believe what you want. I still don't understand why you are here harassing me."

"I'm harassing you?" he exclaims. "You ruined my life. You turned my wife against me."

"If Candy finally stood up to you, that's good, but it's hardly my fault."

"She was just fine until you came along." He begins pacing my small porch.

"Was she?"

He turns suddenly, his face growing dark. "She was. Don't you insinuate otherwise."

"I saw the way you treated her when we were at your house, and I'm sure there were worse times when no one was looking."

"What we do in private is our business," he hisses, moving closer to the cracked door, slowly, deliberately.

"None of this is my business."

His hand suddenly slips through the inches of open door and grabs my hair.

"Then why did you make it your business and turn my wife against me?" he hisses, so close I can smell the alcohol on his breath.

I pull away until my scalp stings, but he won't let go.

"Get your hands off me," I hiss back.

He pulls forward suddenly, and my face slams into the back of the door. Pain shoots from my nose and through my head.

I feel hot blood spurt onto my upper lip.

He still holds my hair, but I pull back far enough to undo the chain.

"How dare you come here and attack me," I shout, as the door opens enough for me to get through. He is so surprised that I'm coming for him, he lets go of my hair and turns away.

I jump onto his back, knocking him over. "This is my house," I shout, clawing at his face.

We roll into the grass, me scratching him, him pulling on my arms. He's not a big man, but he's larger than me. After several moments, he manages to get me pinned to the ground. He straddles my waist, his hands holding my shoulders down.

In the glow of the porch light, he looks like a madman.

"You should have stayed away from my wife," he says, low and menacing.

"You shouldn't have come here," I reply. Putting as much force as I can behind it, I lift my knee fast into his groin.

He didn't see the knee coming and collapses in pain on top of me.

I push him off and regain my feet, ready to keep fighting. He holds himself and rolls on the ground. I wipe my dripping nose. The sight of my blood on my hand fills me with rage.

I kick him in the back. "You should have stayed away," I shout.

I need to call the police, but my phone is back in my room. I see the outline of his in his back pocket. I pull it out and dial 911.

After I tell them what happened, I drop the phone on the grass. Antonio is still holding himself, looking up at me.

"You move before the police get here for you, I swear I will kick you there again," I say, panting in excitement and fear.

He stares at me with dark eyes of hatred. I look away, but keep my attention on his movements. All the fight seems to have left him.

Several tense moments pass and then a squad car pulls up to my curb. Officer James Frazier climbs out.

My heart sinks. I am not Frazier's favorite person.

"Rylan," Frazier says stiffly, looking at Antonio on the ground. "What's going on here?"

"This man came here yelling at me about his wife kicking him out. Then he grabbed my hair and smashed my face into the door." I wipe at my nose and show him the blood.

Frazier stands with his thumbs tucked into his belt, watching Antonio as he climbs to his feet. "Is that true? Did you assault Rylan?"

"I didn't do anything. She just went crazy and kicked me."

"He had me pinned to the ground when I kicked him there. I had to defend myself."

Frazier looks at my bloodied face and then to Antonio. "Why are you here?"

"She—she. Oh, never mind. Just take me in." He seems to crumple.

"His wife finally got the nerve to kick him out and he blames me. It's his fault for being so awful to her."

"You do this kind of thing to your wife?" Frazier asks, all bristles now.

"I didn't do anything," Antonio denies, looking at the ground.

"You want to press charges?" Frazier asks me.

"For sure, I do."

"But she kicked me," Antonio cries.

"Only because you came here drunk and attacked me," I protest.

Frazier has it in for me and I'd been a little afraid he wouldn't believe my story. My fears were unfounded, though. He takes cuffs from his belt and tells Antonio to turn around. I smother a smile.

"You're under arrest for assault," Frazier says, then leads Antonio to his cruiser. After shutting Antonio in the car, Frazier returns.

"You'll have to fill out a report," he says.

"That's fine," I say. Only then do I notice the night chill. I'm dressed in only a tank top and shorts, my usual sleeping attire.

Frazier notices my shiver. "Do you want to go get a jacket first?"

Who would have thought, James Frazier could be nice to me after all.

I hurry into the house and find a jacket and a pair of sweats. I come back outside and fill out the required paperwork to put Antonio in jail for what he did to me.

Frazier tucks the papers into his pocket, then asks, "Do you need medical attention? You have a lot of blood on your face."

I touch my nose, checking if it's broken. "It aches something terrible, but it doesn't feel broken. I think I'll be okay."

Frazier looks at me with concern. "You go to the hospital and have that looked at if anything changes."

I'm not used to him being so nice, but I'll take it. Truth is I'm a little shook up now that the adrenaline is wearing off.

"Thanks, Jimmy," I say sincerely.

He smiles warmly, not the usual scowl he has when he's arresting me. I prefer this version of Officer Frazier.

TWENTY-NINE

BESS

Earlier

I don't see Jacob again for what must be several days. There are no clocks in this underground hell. There are no windows to see the sun, to mark the time.

There is only silence.

Silence and Missy.

I do my best not to upset her. I do my best to care for her.

I've never been a mother, and I don't even have nieces or nephews. I am not cut out for this job.

But I get the feeling my life depends on it.

Missy makes vague references to previous "mommies" to scare me.

It works. Nearly everything she does scares me.

I wonder what happened to her to make her this way. She is so young. Once in a while, I'll watch her playing with her mountain of toys and believe she is just a young girl, innocent and trusting.

She'll feel me watching, her head turning slowly, the lopsided grin a pink slice in her face.

The eyes are not innocent.

I always have to look away with a shudder.

My duties to care for Missy don't take up too much time, and I often find myself sitting at the kitchen table with nothing to do. The small space we live in only takes so long to clean. Making food from the canned goods and freeze-dried foodstuffs is easy and takes barely any time.

In the first days of being locked in here, I searched for a book to read, a magazine, anything to pass the time.

Nothing.

So I sit and rub my fingernail into a scratch on the Formica tabletop.

And imagine a way out of here.

Jacob came and went without opening the trap door. There has to be a secret passage or something.

At night, when Missy is asleep, I search for it. There are few walls in this bunker, few places a secret door could be.

I've never found it.

So I sit and listen to the silence, broken by the clacking of Missy's toys from her room, the occasional word she exclaims.

I rub the scratch harder, pushing my fingernail into it until it hurts.

The pain reminds me I'm alive.

I have a life worth fighting for.

The soft sounds of Missy playing stop suddenly.

"Mommy?" she calls.

I jump to my feet, almost relieved to have something to do. Anything to fill the time.

"Yes, Missy?" I ask, leaning into her room.

"Have you seen my puppet?"

I didn't even know she had a puppet. I scan the piles of toys, the crowded shelves, the overflowing toy box.

"Where's the last place you had it?"

Her tiny pink lips purse. "If I knew that, I'd know where it is," she says menacingly.

I take an involuntary step back. "Of course." I force my lips to smile. "Let's find it together."

I make my feet step into her room. I check the shelves first, not turning my back on her. I feel her eyes watching me search. "What does this puppet look like?"

"It has a top hat and big eyes. It's my favorite. You have to find it."

I'm not the one that lost it, but I don't point that out. "Don't worry, we'll find it real quick."

The puppet is not on her shelves, nor is it in the piles of toys on the floor. I even empty the whole toy box, but no puppet.

When I've looked everywhere, I stand and scan the room again. "I'm sorry, Missy, I don't think it's in here."

I brace for her reaction.

She balls her fists a moment and I wonder if she is going to hit me.

Then she looks like she is listening to something. I listen, too, but all I hear is the silence. The ever-present silence.

"There you are, silly," she says, jumping onto the bed and pulling the covers back. In the middle of the bed, well-hidden by the purple comforter, is the ugliest puppet I've ever seen.

Its head is made of papier-mâché, with harsh features and a prominent nose. The eyes are too big for the head, the head too big for the cloth body that fits over the hand. It wears a top hat, set on an angle.

It does not look like something a little girl would enjoy playing with. But Missy is not your typical little girl.

She snuggles onto the bed with the toy on her hand. She makes it talk into her ear, smiles, giggles, looks up at me.

"Mr. Puppet says you are not very smart. You didn't find his hiding place."

I take an instant dislike to Mr. Puppet. "Tell him he is just too good a hider;" I try to play along, although my skin crawls.

Missy grows serious. "He can hear you."

"I'm sorry. Hello, Mr. Puppet," I try again.

"He says get out. He doesn't want to play with you." Her voice is low.

I take a step toward the door.

A moment of panic crosses her face, making me stop.

"Please," she whispers, sincerely concerned, her expression that of a frightened child. "You have to go. Hurry."

As I watch, her face grows hard again. "Get out!" she shouts.

I hurry from the room and shut the door behind me.

I stand in the main room, confused.

Behind Missy's door, I hear murmured conversation of what sounds like two people. Is she playing with the puppet, making her voice different for his parts?

I press my ear to her door, trying to hear.

The voices stop, but not before I hear what sounds like the word, "kill."

I pull away from the door and rush to my room. I shut my door behind me, wishing I had a lock.

The murmuring conversation begins again, but I can't make out any words.

I curl onto my cot and cover my ears with the thin pillow.

Now all I can hear is silence. An ever-present, oppressive silence.

THIRTY

RYLAN FLYNN

After my late night with Antonio Carrillo, I truly need a bear claw this morning. The scent of cooked pastries fills my nose when I enter The Hole. I breathe deeply, feeling a weight shift from my shoulders. I am the only patron in the shop.

Aunt Val is behind the counter and hands me my bear claw before I even ask for it. I take the wax-papered confection eagerly.

"Late night?" she asks with a knowing look.

I take a bite and let the cinnamon and sugar melt on my tongue before I answer. She probably already knows about Antonio. Not much happens in this town that doesn't get discussed inside these old brick walls.

"You heard about that man coming to my house?" I ask after I swallow.

"It was mentioned here this morning. Officer Ramone came in and asked about you. I pretended to know what was up, but, of course, you didn't call me so I didn't know."

"It was late and it wasn't a big deal."

"That's why your nose is bruised."

"Is it?" I ask, my hand flying to my face. It definitely ached when I woke up but I didn't see any bruising.

"Just a little. Most people wouldn't notice."

The bell above the door jingles and a couple enters. I take my usual table by the front window, watching people come and go across the street at the court house. A few raindrops hit the glass and dribble down. It had been sunny when I entered. Typical changing Indiana weather.

The people walking into the courthouse quicken their steps to get out of the sudden rain.

Aunt Val helps the couple, and, once they are settled at their own table, she joins me with two coffees. "So, want to tell me what happened or should I get Officer Ramone back in here?"

I take a quick look over my shoulder at the other couple. They are more interested in each other than in what I might say. In a low voice, I say, "It all started with a séance."

Val is all ears as I tell her about Sarah being murdered and helping her cross over. Halfway through my story, the couple leaves and we can talk more freely.

"You really called her mother back from the other side?" she asks.

I give a self-satisfied smile. "We did."

"How does that tie in with your bruised nose?"

I explain how Antonio got upset when Candy kicked him out. "Serves him right. He was a piece of work."

"Tall guy, dark hair, and bushy eyebrows?" Val asks.

"You know him?"

"He comes in here with his wife. He's a bit overbearing. I can see why she'd leave him."

"He wasn't too nice last night when he grabbed my hair and slammed my face into the door."

Val sits forward. "He didn't?"

"He did. But I got him back. I kicked him real hard." I point down.

Val's eyebrows lift. "Good girl."

A man enters the shop and Val jumps up to help him. I watch the rain grow in intensity, splattering on the picture window. The wind is picking up.

The man takes his donuts and waits at the door. He opens it an inch or two and the growing wind blows through the crack, sending my napkin flying.

"Either in or out, Gene," Val says good-naturedly, coming back around the counter and picking up my napkin.

"Think I'll make a run for it," he says over his shoulder and darts into the rain. A woman ducks in as he leaves, shaking water from the hood of her jacket. I'm surprised to see Candy Carrillo.

"Candy?"

"Rylan, I thought that was your car out front. Figured I jump in here and see." She stands next to our table awkwardly.

"We were just discussing what happened last night. Are you okay?"

Candy stands tall. "I'm better than okay. I was just at the courthouse to file for divorce."

"Oh, Candy, I'm sorry."

"Sorry? Heck no. For the first time in a long time, I can see freedom."

I scoot over in the booth, offer her a seat. "What happened?"

"Well, last night, as you know, he came out bellowing as usual. He was rude to you guys and, I don't know. Something just snapped."

She rubs a drip of water from her forehead, pushes her wet bangs back. "I thought to myself, *I can't do this anymore.* You saw what he's like. He's often much worse."

A cloud crosses her features, then quickly passes.

"Anyway, I just couldn't take it anymore. I told him we were through and we started fighting something fierce. I said I couldn't live with an abusive man, especially one who's descended from a murderer."

"Oh no," I breathe.

"Yep. You should have seen him lose it." She shifts in her seat, the excitement dampened a bit. "He threw his beer bottle at the fireplace, nearly hit me instead. I wouldn't let him win, though." Her voice has the slightest waver. "I told him to leave."

"That had to be scary," Val says gently.

Candy looks at Val, takes a deep breath. "It was. I was sure he was going to come after me." She looks to me. "I guess he went after you instead."

I rub my sore nose, self-consciously. "That's okay. He's locked up for now."

She pushes back in the booth. "For now. In the meantime, I'm packing up his stuff and putting it on the porch. Oh, and there's the restraining order I applied for this morning." She adds it like an afterthought, but I can tell she's upset.

"You're doing the right thing," Val says.

"I know." Candy pushes her bangs back again. "It's just all so new."

"You can do this," I say, reaching for her damp hands.

"My sister is coming to stay with me for a few days. That should help."

"I'm glad you're not going to be alone," I say. "Let me know if you need anything or if I can help."

Candy smiles wide. "You've already helped more than you know." She pushes her hands flat on the table and stands. "I've got to go. Like I said, I saw that car of yours and wanted to tell you what's going on."

"I'm glad you're doing okay."

She lifts her chin. "It will take some time, but I'll be more than okay."

She nods to us both in turn, then ducks out into the rain.

"I should be going, too. I'm supposed to do voiceovers with Mickey today." I make my way to the door, look outside into the rain.

"So, the show's going well?" Val says.

"Mickey says we are getting more and more viewers. We even lined up a new sponsor last week."

"That's good, right?"

"Yeah, but that's Mickey's area of expertise." I give her a quick hug goodbye.

Luckily, I'm parked right out front on the curb, so I don't get too wet running to my car. I slide into the front seat and turn on the wipers. They screech back and forth. I blast the defroster to remove the fog from the inside of the windshield as I drive home.

The rain and wind blast the car, pushing me sideways.

"Holy flip," I say as I fight to keep the car on the road.

Suddenly, the car lurches and I hear a loud bang.

There's a flapping sound as loose rubber beats against the wheel well.

I groan and put my head down on the steering wheel.

I have a flat tire in the biggest rainstorm we've seen in a month.

THIRTY-ONE

FORD PIERCE

The coffee from the gas station near the precinct is just awful. I return the still-full cup to the cupholder in my car, wishing I had stopped at The Hole this morning. Val's coffee is ten times better. The files on the passenger seat slide off to the floor as I turn into the parking lot.

Bess Freeman's file flips open and her dimpled smile seems to glare at me. It makes me sick that I haven't found her yet. We're still no closer and a deep dread has seeped its way into my bones. If we don't find her soon, I fear we never will.

I reach for the awful coffee; any caffeine is better than none.

Something slams into the driver's window and I jerk, spilling the awful brew all over the center console.

"Sitting here drinking coffee while my cousin is missing?" Kaitlyn demands from the other side of the glass.

I scramble for napkins to clean the spill while I roll down the window.

"Jeez, Kaitlyn, look what you did."

She eyes the spilled coffee, but her tight expression doesn't waver. "Do you have any new information?"

I sop up the coffee and toss the soggy napkins into the back-seat. "We're doing all we can. I wish I had more for you," I say, sounding lame even to myself.

"That's the same line you've been giving me. You have to find her." Her voice softens a notch.

"Barreling over here and making me spill my coffee is not going to find her any faster."

I wipe the last of the spill and turn my full attention to her. I remind myself she's the victim's family, not just my ex.

"Look, Kaitlyn. We really are doing what we can. There just isn't much to go on." As I get out of the car, a fellow officer walks by, eyeing us curiously. I feel exposed, confronted by Kaitlyn in such a public place.

"What about that man she left with? You find him yet?" The wind has picked up and her hair blows wildly.

"All we have is a vague description and a video that doesn't show his face." I don't know why I feel so defensive.

Kaitlyn backs away from my open door. "I can't do this." Her voice breaks into a slight slur. "Everyone at work is now looking at me like I have something to do with her disappearance. I heard your boy Tyler was there snooping around."

She lifts her eyes to mine, daring me to look away. I let her win and drop my eyes.

"Yes, he went to your offices. It was all routine." I school my face into a placid expression.

"Routine?" She studies me with the same unnerving attention she used to use on me when she thought I was up to something. I never was, but that didn't stop her from scrutinizing my every move. "You sent him. You really think I might have done something to Bess?"

"Did you?" The words dart from my lips before I can stop them. Rain begins to drop on my face.

"You know I didn't!" she exclaims. "How dare you!" She flies at me, stumbling. I catch her by the wrists. This close, I can smell the alcohol on her breath. "It's early for drinking, too early," I say gently.

She collapses against my chest. "I don't care. All I care about is finding Bess." Lightning slices through the sky nearby, making us both jump.

Tyler is hurrying up the sidewalk, his head lowered to the rain that is falling in earnest now. He looks at us together, questions all over his face. I motion with my chin for him to leave as Kaitlyn breaks into a sob. He silently backs away.

I let her cry it out, conscious of the others hurrying in the parking lot, wondering what they are thinking of our little show. I push her away a few inches. "How about I take you home?" I say gently. "You shouldn't be driving."

"I drove here," she points out, a little unsteady on her feet.

"That doesn't mean you should have."

She bows her head, conceding, and lets me lead her around to the passenger side.

Once we are settled in my Malibu, I pull into traffic. "I'll take you home. Can you get a ride back for your car later?"

She runs a finger through the condensation on the passenger window and nods. She writes BESS on the window. "You will find her, right?" she asks miserably.

I don't want to tell her about my doubts. Every day that passes puts Bess in more danger. If she isn't already dead, she may soon be.

"We will," I say with as much conviction as I can muster. I shouldn't be making promises, but I feel I have to. I hate seeing Kaitlyn like this.

The wipers sway back and forth, the rhythmic sound soothing. "Man, it's really raining," I say to fill the quiet.

Kaitlyn suddenly sits up, leaning toward the windshield. "Isn't that the ghost girl?" she asks, a sharp edge to her words that I don't like.

I squint through the rain and see Rylan's boat of a car on the side of the road. "Does she have a flat?" I say. Rylan kneels next to the back driver's side wheel well with a tire tool in her hand.

I pull up next to her and run the window down.

THIRTY-TWO

RYLAN FLYNN

I'm completely drenched by the time I get the spare out of the trunk and the car jacked up. My hair is plastered to my head, long rivulets of water slide down my face. I manage to loosen the first two lug nuts, but the third one gives me fits. I pull on the tire iron with all my weight, but it won't budge. I sit back on my heels and stare at it in frustration.

A car pulls up next to me. A black Malibu with chrome trim.

Ford's car.

My heart speeds up as the passenger window rolls down. I stand, put on my most winning smile, and turn.

And see Kaitlyn staring at me with disdain.

The smile slides off my face.

"You got a flat," Kaitlyn says, pointing out the obvious.

"Yeah, I know."

"You need help?" Ford leans toward the window, very close to Kaitlyn.

"I got it," I lie.

"Looked like that lug nut was giving you trouble," he says. "Let me help."

Before I can protest further, he pulls in front of my car and parks on the side of the road.

Rain runs through his super short dark hair, soaking him before he even reaches my car.

"You don't have to do this," I yell into the wind.

"Can't leave you stranded out here."

"What about Kaitlyn?" I ask, handing him the tire iron.

He looks back to his car. "She can wait."

I like that answer.

He crouches and cranks on the lug nut. I'm not surprised when it loosens on the second try.

"I got the others, but that one was really sticking," I say, crouching next to him. He hands it to me and starts on the last one. That one comes off easily.

"You really did a number on this tire," he says rolling the destroyed tire away and replacing it with the spare.

"It just kind of blew," I say.

"The tread is thread bare," he says. "See?"

I lean closer than necessary to look. "Yeah, this car's been around a while."

He looks at the front tire. "You might want to get new ones. That one is pretty bad, too. Just a matter of time until it gives out."

I can't believe I'm crouching in the rain talking about tires with Ford. The whole thing feels like a dream.

Kaitlyn honks the horn, and the dream-like quality disappears.

"So, you and Kaitlyn?" I can't stop the question.

He doesn't look up from tightening the last lug. "She showed up in the parking lot, upset about Bess."

"Oh."

He stops twirling the tire iron and leans in close. "She's been drinking," he says quietly. "I couldn't let her drive home." I revel in the conspiratorial tone.

"I'll keep her secret," I say, pleased beyond belief that there's a simple reason they are in his car together. "You're nice to drive her home."

"I didn't have a choice. I need to be working, but it won't take long."

"How is the case coming? You any closer to finding Bess?" I ask, serious now.

He cranks hard on the last nut, harder than necessary. "No. I'm waiting on the tech guys to finish with her computer, but really I'm not holding out much hope there." He sits back on his heels and turns his wet face to mine. "I'm a little worried."

The fear behind his eyes hurts my heart. "You'll find her," I try to reassure him.

He holds my eyes a long moment, then gives the nut one last crank. "I hope you're right." He stands and so do I, wiping my hands down my damp jeans.

"What about the body Jamie found? Any headway there?"

His expression grows clouded. "Not really. We have a name, Lynette Reed, and that's about all. Pretty sure her husband, Jacob, killed her and took off. We've tried everything and can't find him. It's like he just disappeared."

"I'm sorry. I wish I could help more."

"You've helped a lot." He holds my eyes with his. I'm suddenly not chilled by the rain.

We stand like that for a heavy moment. Then the horn honks again, shattering the mood.

He darts his eyes to his car. "I should probably get her home," he says.

"Yeah, probably." He hands me the tire iron and bends to lift the blown tire.

"Let me put this back first."

I let the car down off the jack and carry it to the trunk. I left it open an inch and he lifts the hatch.

My trunk is full of things. He smiles when he sees the mess.

"How did you even get the spare out of here?" he asks, good-naturedly.

"Easy, I just took everything out first. Just toss that stuff in and I'll put it away later." I shift stuff so there's room for the tire and the tools.

He lugs the tire into the cavernous trunk. I add the jack and tire iron and shut it.

"See, easy," I say.

He stares at me a long moment, shaking his head.

"You're something," he says, making my heart trip.

"Because my car is a mess?"

He shakes his head a little. "You're just you. I like that."

He likes that.

He reaches for my cheek, wipes away a drop of rain, leaving a trail of heat where he touches.

Kaitlyn yells out the window for him to hurry up.

He looks toward the car and back to me. "I gotta go."

"Thanks again."

He makes no move to leave.

"Ford?" Kaitlyn calls.

Without another word, he leaves and drives away.

I slog through the rain back to my seat. Once out of the rain, I realize how wet I am. My clothes are completely soaked, my hair dripping. I rummage through the crowded backseat and find a towel to dry my hair.

Ford's tail lights disappear into the rain.

I take a deep breath and touch my cheek where he touched it.

So close.

I push thoughts of Ford to where I usually keep them. Way in the back of my mind. Mickey needs my full attention today, as does

Bess and the murders. I spend the afternoon and early evening doing voiceovers for the show about Sarah. Earlier today, Mickey went back to the cemetery and got some nice shots to use for B-roll. Close-ups of Sarah and her parents' graves, the cemetery. Between these and the shots she got of me talking to spirits the other night, we have plenty of footage to edit together a good show.

When we are done, I push the microphone away and lean back in my chair.

"Glad that's done," I say with relief. I don't mind being on camera when I'm at a location and with a spirit. This talking, narrating, feels foreign to me, even after all the shows we've done. "Maybe you should take over the voiceovers," I say like I do every time.

Mickey doesn't even respond. We've been over it plenty. I'm the face of the show. Mickey likes being behind the camera, not on it.

"I'll have this all put together by tomorrow," she says.

"You're the best. I don't know how you do all you do," I say sincerely.

"Teamwork. Don't forget that."

I pull my hair out of the hair tie I shoved it in when I arrived. It's still damp, reminding me of my encounter with Ford in the rain. I smile to myself.

Mickey sees.

"What's up? You have a strange smile."

I tell her about the flat tire and how Ford helped me. She listens with a knowing look. She's known since high school about my feelings for Ford. Ever since I used to write *Mrs. Rylan Pierce* on my notebook.

"Too bad he had Kaitlyn with him," I add. "She's the worst." I instantly feel bad. The woman is going through a lot right now.

"This has got to be hard on her," Mickey says, always the peacemaker.

"Yeah, I know. I should be nicer." I finger the charms on my bracelet. "Do you think they'll find Bess?"

Mickey seriously thinks about the question. "I don't know, honestly. The odds aren't good. What is it that they say about the chances of solving a crime after the first 48 hours?"

"I feel so responsible. I was the last one to see her. I saw the man she left with. The man that most likely took her."

"You can't blame yourself. You didn't kidnap her."

"No. I suppose not."

"Let's go over what you remember. Maybe something new will come up."

I rub the cross charm on my bracelet between my fingers and close my eyes. "Lord, let me see something," I say quickly, then focus on the memory.

"She fell out of the door and her braid hit me in the face," I start. "She was with a man, but I didn't get a good look at him. I was focused on Bess."

"What happened then?"

I squeeze my eyes tight, thinking, praying. "They walked away across the parking lot. I was worried they were too drunk to drive."

"Okay, which way did they go?"

"To the south. I never did hear a car, but maybe they left after I went inside."

"Or they walked home."

"I thought they walked at the time." I hold the cross charm of my bracelet in my fingers.

"Did you tell Ford this?"

"That I didn't hear them drive away? No."

"Maybe you should. It could mean something."

"What could it mean? They probably just started the car after I went inside. I only waited a moment. Besides, the first thing the cops would do is canvas the neighborhood."

"But they didn't find anything."

"Nope."

Mickey looks concerned. "So it's a dead end."

"I guess."

"What are you going to do?"

"What can I do? It's not like Bess's ghost has come calling. I hope she's still on this side and with us and not a spirit yet." This triggers something in the back of my mind.

Mickey squeezes my arm. "I'm sure she is. Now stop blaming yourself."

I look out the window and it's growing dark. "I should be going."

"Yeah. I have these voiceovers to add in, too."

"You going to work on those tonight?"

"Marco is on a late shift. I might as well get them done."

I give Mickey a quick hug and then let myself out the front door. I'm almost home when I realize that, even though I was there for hours, I didn't see the little boy ghost.

THIRTY-THREE

BESS

Earlier

Missy starts taking the puppet with her everywhere. When we eat, he sits on the table next to her plate. His huge, uncanny eyes stare at me while I try to swallow. He sits on her lap while she watches cartoons. She even takes him to the bathroom with her, and sleeps with him in her bed.

Often I hear them talking in low voices. Missy making his parts deep and gravelly. I don't think her connection with the puppet is healthy, but I am terrified of what Missy might do if I try to get between them.

I think it is afternoon. It's after lunch. The only way I can mark time is by when we get hungry or when we get tired. The lack of time is slowly driving me mad. This "afternoon," Missy watches a movie with Mr. Puppet on her lap.

"She really loves Mr. Puppet," Jacob says near my shoulder.

I jump and spin around, my heart hammering. I clutch my chest in surprise. "Where did you come from?"

The TV is on, but it's not really loud. It's not loud enough to cover the sound of him coming down the stairs. Or is it?

"You shouldn't let her play with him so much." Jacob ignores my question, his eyes locked on Missy.

She doesn't turn, acts like she doesn't even hear him.

"How am I supposed to stop her?"

"That puppet is not safe."

He walks around the couch and kneels in front of Missy. She finally acknowledges his presence.

"Daddy!" she squeals. I expect her to throw her arms around him, but she just bounces on the cushions. "You came. Where've you been?"

"Sorry. I couldn't come earlier. You know it's hard for me to get here."

I watch his face as he watches his daughter. His eyes are full of love and something else.

Fear?

Missy crosses her arms and pouts. "Mr. Puppet doesn't like it when you're gone so long."

"Mr. Puppet should know why I can't come more often," he says stiffly.

What is it with this family and this puppet?

"He knows lots of things," she whispers.

Jacob seems at a loss for words to that. He looks at me then back to Missy. "Maybe you should put Mr. Puppet away for a while."

She grabs the toy and wraps her arms around it. "No." One firm word.

He looks defeated, pleads with me with his eyes.

"Missy, maybe he can play alone in your room while you visit with your dad," I offer, standing.

Missy turns slowly to face me. "You don't get a say," she hisses. I should be used to Missy's strange turns of mood, but this time there's a threat under her words. I take an involuntary step back and bump into the wall.

"She's scared of us," she says to the puppet. She holds it to her ear, listening. She then smiles the crooked grin I've learned to hate. If I could back up further, I would.

I'm so focused on Missy that I don't realize that Jacob has snuck out of the room.

"Where did he go?" I ask once I see I'm alone with the girl and the toy.

"She still doesn't get it," Missy says to the puppet, then turns back to her movie.

"Seriously, how did he leave?" I begin searching the walls for the secret entrance. I even look up the stairs to make sure the trap door is closed. I run up the stairs and push on the metal. It doesn't budge.

"Let me out!" I shout, banging on the door.

"Shut up!" Missy screams. "Just shut up or we'll kill you."

I crumble onto the top step.

I believe her threat.

"God, please help me," I begin praying, because only God can help me now.

THIRTY-FOUR

RYLAN FLYNN

I sit on a chair in Mom's room, the TV in the corner on. I'd hoped the familiar activity of watching TV with Mom would soothe my anxiety. Not even a *Parks and Recreation* re-run can distract me.

I'm worried about Bess.

I'm worried about Miss Melanie and Lynette.

I'm worried for the safety of my town.

I shift in the chair, trying to get comfortable.

"Do you want to watch something else?" Mom asks.

"No. Why?"

"Because you keep sighing and shifting. I like this episode, but we can change it if you want."

I stretch my back, but it doesn't relieve the tension. "I should be doing something."

"Leave it to Ford and Tyler," she says. I'm surprised she remembers what I told her about the cases.

"You're right." I lean back and try to focus on the show. It's a lost cause. I jump up. "I'm going to get some air."

I make my way down the paths of the house and out onto the back patio. The night is mild, with just the tiniest nip in the air. I rub my arms, wishing I had grabbed a jacket. I look at the flickering light from Mom's window and debate going back inside.

I just can't face being cooped up tonight.

Standing on the edge of the concrete patio, I look up into the stars. The earlier storm has long since blown away and the sky is wide open, the stars glittering.

"Bess, where are you?" I ask the sky. "Are you still alive?"

On impulse, I throw my arms wide, my palms up and call to her spirit. "If you're out there and stuck on this side, come to me," I whisper into the breeze.

I focus all my attention on reaching Bess. I bring up the memory of her face from when she ran into me. I think of the picture Kaitlyn showed us.

I don't know the woman, but I feel a connection to her.

I hope the connection is enough to pull her spirit to me.

With all my attention focused on her, I plead with the universe.

But I don't get any tingles.

I don't get anything.

The window to Keaton's old room is directly behind me. Through the glass, I hear laughter.

I drop my arms, feeling scared and foolish. Turning away from the window, I slink back inside the house. The walls and piles of stuff instantly encompass me. Normally that sensation is soothing. Tonight it feels oppressive.

I duck into Mom's room to tell her I'm heading out. The TV is on, but Mom isn't there now. I stare at the empty bed, a deep loneliness sinking into me. With a sigh, I switch the TV off. The room is dark. So is my mood.

I grab a jacket from my room and head out the front door. I don't normally drink much, but tonight I want people around me and a vodka tonic.

The lights of The Lock Up spill onto the street, the music

thumping through the walls. I park in the lot in back and hurry to the entrance. At the door, I hesitate, reliving my momentary encounter with Bess.

She had definitely been drinking, that much I think I know. She was so out of it, I wonder now if she had been drugged. I should have intervened. I should have done something, anything. I could have saved her.

I pull the door open in frustration.

The music and talking envelop me, and I don't feel so alone.

I make my way through the crowd to the bar and find an open seat. The same bartender that was here last time approaches. She doesn't recognize me, but gives me a friendly enough greeting and a napkin.

I order a vodka tonic and play with the napkin. Now that I'm here, I feel a little out of place. Last time, I was with Ford. Now I feel vulnerable.

I push the thought away and listen to the music. There's no band tonight, but the speakers are blaring 1990s alternative. I nod along with Green Day and accept my drink with a half-hearted smile.

After several minutes and several sips, I start to relax. I take a deep breath and feel the tension leave my shoulders.

Then I feel the tingle in my back.

I look into the mirror behind the bar, wondering where the spirit is, but not wanting it to know I've sensed it.

It's impossible.

The room is full of people.

I try to ignore the tingle and focus on my drink, keeping my head down.

The tingle grows stronger and I turn in my seat to scan the crowd. A few men see me looking around and offer tentative smiles. I nod at each one, then quickly look away so they don't take it as an invitation.

Then I see him.

He looks vaguely familiar.

He's standing behind a group at a table in the corner, his back against the wall. He's watching me with intense interest.

He smiles when he sees me watching him. A memory flits through my mind. He's the man I talked with briefly at the scene where they found Melanie Shaw's bones.

I had thought there was a spirit there at the time.

It was him.

I nod at him and he disappears.

Only to reappear next to me.

"You can see me," he says near my ear.

I nod and take a drink from my glass.

"Why is that? No one else here can ever see me."

"I'm not everyone else," I say, hoping no one notices I'm talking to myself.

He looks around the room, understands the problem. "Want to go outside so we can talk? No one ever talks to me."

He seems so sad and sincere, my curiosity gets the better of me. I down my drink and sit the empty on the bar. I then push through the crowd and out the door.

"So why can you see me?" he asks when we are outside and alone. "Sometimes I can make people see me if I try really hard, but it takes a lot of energy and I can't do it very long. I'm not even trying now."

"I just can. I saw you at the crime scene the other day too."

"I remember. You kind of freaked me out when you answered me."

"I didn't realize then what you were."

"So you can see people like me?"

"Yes. That's what I do. I help the souls that are stuck here. Do you know why you are still here?"

He grows serious. "Yes, I know why. And you can't help me."

"I have helped lots of you to cross over. My partner Mickey and me and my dad. We do it all the time."

"I can't cross over. I have work to do here."

"What kind of work?" I ask, wondering what could be more important than crossing over.

"I have to take care of my daughter."

"From the beyond?"

"Yes. It's the least I can do."

A moment of silence fills the parking lot. "I'm Rylan Flynn, by the way."

The mood shifts and he smiles. "I'm Jacob Reed. Nice to meet you."

THIRTY-FIVE

RYLAN FLYNN

Reed.

Miss Melanie called for a Reed when she got scared and he was at her crime scene.

And Lynette's last name was Reed.

I back away from the ghost, my instincts suddenly on high alert.

"How are you related to Lynette Reed?" I blurt out.

He seems shocked at the name. "Lynette? How do you know her?"

"Her body was found the other day. Holy flip, you're her husband." I back further away, but he steps closer.

"What do you mean her body was found?" he asks in a panic.

"She was found in a cabinet in your old house. You should know, you put her there." I make a wild accusation, curious about his reaction.

"I didn't know she was found. This isn't good." He rubs his face.

"That's an understatement. Wait. You said you have to take care of your daughter. Where is she?"

Jacob is no longer there. I'm alone in the parking lot, talking to myself.

I fish my phone out of my pocket and dial Ford before I even realize it. "Are you still looking for Jacob Reed?" I ask without saying hello.

"Yes. So far, we haven't had any luck."

"That's because he's dead. I just talked to his ghost."

"Really? Where?"

"At The Lock Up. He was here and surprised I could see him. He said he is here still because he has to take care of his daughter. He also didn't protest when I said he killed Lynette."

"Is he still there?" he asks, excited.

"No. He got upset about Lynette being found. He didn't know about it. Then he disappeared."

His voice suddenly turns softer. "Are you okay?"

Am I?

"Yes. I think so. Except I just talked to a killer." I pace around the parking lot, my adrenaline high.

"You still at the bar?"

"I'm in the parking lot."

"You should go home."

I stop my pacing. He's right, but I'm not about to tell him that. "I might," I hedge. I don't feel like going home.

"It's not safe if Jacob is there."

"He's a ghost. What can he do?"

"He's a killer."

"In life. He's dead now." That fact suddenly hits home. "He's dead. And he's here." I spin around slowly, as if the answer will suddenly appear in the parking lot. "Where is his body?"

"Rylan, I recognize that tone," Ford says with warning. "You stay out of this."

I keep spinning, feeling the air on my skin, searching for tingles. I ignore his warning. "Do you remember how I told you that I never heard Bess and the man that took her drive away?"

"Yes..."

"What if they walked? That would mean Bess would be close by. If Jacob's ghost is here, that would mean he could be close by, too."

"What are you getting at?" I hear his keys jangle and picture him grabbing his jacket.

"They are related."

"That's a stretch."

I feel the vaguest tingle at the base of my spine. "I think I'm right." I turn in the direction I think the tingle is coming from.

"Don't do anything. You can't go looking for them."

"I'm just going to go for a little walk. You come join me. I saw them leave south, so that's the way I'm going."

"Ry, you've got to wait for me."

"You're only a few minutes away. I won't go far before you get here."

I hang up before Ford can argue further. The vodka is giving me just enough liquid courage to go looking.

The tiny tingle in my back grows as I make my way down the sidewalk. I expect to see Ford's car any moment, but besides a truck pulling into the bar's parking lot, the street is empty.

I look right and left as I make my way, all the while paying attention to the growing tingle. At the corner, I start to cross the street, but the tingling fades. I turn right and it increases.

I continue on this way for another few blocks, turning when I need to, going straight when the tingle stays the same. I eventually find myself in a residential neighborhood near the Lutheran preschool and its playground.

Wondering if Ford will ever be able to find me after all the turning, I stop in front of the school. When I walk past it, the sensation fades. When I return, it grows.

"Jacob?" I call into the darkness of the playground. The

breeze picks up and the swings begin moving on their own. I start toward the swings, but the feeling in my back grows weaker.

I return to the sidewalk and turn around. Where should I go? Dark houses line the streets. Only one porch light on. I suddenly feel very alone, but I'm not. I feel eyes watching me, human eyes.

A handsome man stands on the sidewalk on the other side of the road. "Jacob told me you might come," the man calls across the street.

"Is he here?"

"He was. He may be back. I never know for sure."

"You can see him? Talk to him?" I ask in surprise.

"He's my brother. We have a bond."

I look both ways to make sure it's safe to cross. There are headlights a few blocks away, but otherwise the neighborhood is silent and empty. We are the only two people here.

"You're Jacob's brother? Then you know he's a ghost?" I say as I reach the sidewalk. The man turns away and I recognize the profile.

It's the man I saw with Bess. The man from the videos.

"You lost your mustache," I say.

He rubs his top lip in surprise. "I don't have a mustache."

"You did when you took Bess. Where is she?" I start across the street.

"You know Bess?" We stand together in the pool of light from a street lamp, each of us circling.

"I saw you take her."

"Oh, right. I remember that."

"So, where is she? And where is Jacob? Did you kill him?"

The man laughs, throwing his head back. "I didn't kill him." He grows serious. "I loved him. Still love him."

"If you didn't kill him, who did?"

"Come with me and I will answer all your questions."

"I'm not going anywhere with you." The headlights down the block are growing closer. I wonder if they belong to Ford. I back away from the strange brother onto the lawn of a house.

"Now, you know I can't let you go." His voice had been friendly, kindly even. Now it turns sinister.

I take another step back. The headlights from before are gone.

I'm alone with Bess's kidnapper.

He makes a grab for my arm, but I pull away and run across the yard toward the house.

"Robert, don't let her get away," Jacob shouts from the front steps. I shift my angle and run past the house into the back yard. I wonder if I should scream for help, but I'm running so fast, I can hardly breathe. I doubt there's anyone to hear me anyway.

Robert pounds the grass behind me, gaining ground. In the dark, a detached garage looms in the alley. I see the door and increase my speed to it.

Just as I reach the door of the garage, Robert's hand grabs the back of my shirt and pulls me down. He lands on my back and pulls on my hair.

"You shouldn't have come here." He's close to my ear.

I slam my head backward and feel his nose crunch as my skull crashes into his face. He yelps in pain and lets go of my hair.

I take advantage of the moment and scramble to my feet.

The door leading to the garage is open. I dart inside and slam it behind me. I search for a lock and finally make it latch closed.

I breathe deeply for a moment, as Robert howls in pain outside. "You won't get away with this."

I pull my phone out and hit the speed dial for Ford. "I'm in a garage across from the preschool," I shout into the phone. "Bess's kidnapper is chasing me. It's the brother. Jacob's brother."

Robert pounds on the door, tries the lock.

"I'm just down the block," Ford says.

"Hurry. He's in the alley. I'm inside a garage."

Robert has made his way to the overhead doors and I hear him rattling the handle. I back through the darkness and run into a pickup truck. I don't hang up, but I put the phone back in my pocket and climb under the truck.

The smell of gas and oil fills my nose. I wriggle all the way under the truck, hoping Robert won't find me, but knowing there is probably nowhere else to look in the small garage.

Below me is hard concrete strewn with dirt. Above me, only a scant inch away, is the undercarriage of the truck. I scoot across the concrete as I hear the garage door opening. The ground below me has changed to metal.

I feel the metal with my fingertips and find a handle. And a lock.

It's a trap door.

THIRTY-SIX

BESS

Now

Days pass. At least I think they are days. In the overwhelming silence and absolute dark, I don't know how long has passed. I sleep a lot. There isn't much else to do.

Missy still clings to the puppet.

My hatred of the girl grows with every day.

As does my fear.

Jacob is curiously absent.

Once in a while, Missy will ask about him, but, for the most part, she doesn't really talk.

Neither do I.

I wonder about the others she mentioned. And I wonder about the man that brought me here. It wasn't Jacob. This man was a few years older, and he wore a silly mustache that I had thought was fake but chose to overlook. Why had I been so stupid?

Looking back, I don't know why I left with him. I'd only had two drinks, but I remember being out of it. And then I woke up at the bottom of the stairs.

Drugged. I finally realize I must have been drugged. I never would have gone home with a stranger, no matter how handsome, if I hadn't been seriously intoxicated somehow.

The realization only makes my fear grow.

How long can I live like this? How long did the others last before Missy lost her temper and killed them, like she killed her mother?

Why does Jacob let her get away with it?

Or maybe that's why Missy is here. To hide her from the law.

I don't care why she is here. I just want out.

I daydream all kinds of scenarios where I escape. I hate to admit it, but my favorite is that I take a knife to Missy's throat and demand to be released or I'll cut her. But who would I demand it from? No one else is here.

Jacob has been gone for days.

The man that brought me here hasn't returned.

"It's just me," I mutter from the kitchen table, where I'm once again working on the scratch in the linoleum. I wonder how many other women before me have sat in this chair. Missy is in her room, talking to the puppet as she often does.

I'm sure now that the puppet is telling her to do things.

Last night, I woke to find her over my bed, with the puppet on her hand.

"What are you doing in my room?" I'd asked.

She'd only smiled that lopsided smile and said, "Mr. Puppet doesn't like you."

I was sleepy and not in the mood for her games. "Well, I don't like Mr. Puppet," I'd said.

She'd lost the grin and looked scared. "Don't say that, please don't say that," she'd begged. She seemed so earnest, so not like her usual creepy self, I'd relented. "Of course, I like him," I lied.

This seemed to mollify her. She hasn't talked to me since. She ate her breakfast in silence and returned to her room.

And the day has waned on, slowly, silently. Nothing to help with the passage of time.

I finally can't take it anymore.

I cannot stand being in this room, in this bunker, in this hell another minute.

I must get out.

"Let me out!" I shout, knowing no one can hear me.

Missy comes to the door of her room, looks out, bored. "This again?"

"I want out and I want out now." I jump from my chair, cross the few steps, and tower over her.

Missy gives an exaggerated sigh. Mr. Puppet is on her hand. She puts him to her ear, then laughs. "I know, such a drama queen."

I snap.

And grab the puppet off her hand.

"Give that back," she demands.

"I will if you let me out."

"I can't let you out. If I could, I wouldn't still be in here."

That makes sense. I'd never thought about how Missy felt being locked down here.

"Then let's both get free."

Missy looks bored. "That's impossible, now give him back."

I put the puppet behind my back. "No. You play with him too much."

Missy stomps her foot. "I want him back."

I step away from her. "I'm big and you're little. I said you can't have him."

She rushes into me, pummeling me with her tiny fists. "Give him back! Daddy!"

"Your dad is not coming."

"Uncle Robert," she yells.

"Is that who brought me here? Your uncle, Robert? He told me his name was James."

"Of all the mommies he's brought me, you're the worst," she pouts.

"I'm not in the mood for your opinion, so be quiet," I tell her. She seems pleased by my reaction.

"Mr. Puppet likes you now," she says out of nowhere.

"I'm tired of hearing about Mr. Puppet," I shout. I shake the toy above my head. "No more puppets."

I stomp up the stairs, taking him with me. I pound on the door.

"Let me out or I'll shatter this thing! Robert, let me out."

I have no idea if anyone is out there, but I scream anyway.

"I told you screaming is useless," Missy says from the bottom step. The blade of a knife flashes in her hand.

Is this what she did to the others?

"Where did you get that?"

"I told you, we have everything we need here." She climbs to the third step, entirely too close.

I push on the door again, but it doesn't budge. "Missy, you don't want to do this."

"You should have listened." She slowly climbs up two more steps, close enough to touch my leg now. I kick at her, but she just sinks the knife into my calf, her face split with her lopsided grin.

THIRTY-SEVEN

RYLAN FLYNN

I swear the metal door below me is shaking, or maybe it's just me, shaking in fear. I'm so scared, blood is pumping in my ears.

A muffled scream. "Let me out."

Did I just imagine that?

Robert opens the garage door with a whoosh. Cold air blows under the truck where I am hiding. It's not a good hiding place. He'll find me in a moment.

I listen to his footsteps, trying not to breathe so he can't hear me.

"You really shouldn't be in here," he says. "You shouldn't have come."

I want to move, want to scramble away, but I can't decide what to do.

The door below me vibrates again and a female voice calls for help.

Could that be Bess?

Where is she?

I don't have time to worry about finding her now. I need to save myself.

Robert had been walking around the truck, checking the corners of the dark garage for me.

When the voice cries out, he freezes, his feet a few inches from my face. One of his black sneakers is untied, the string hanging limp.

More banging on the metal door under my belly. More screaming to be released.

"That girl better shut it," Robert says, walking again. He moves to the front of the truck, away from the overhead door. This is my only chance.

As quietly and quickly as possible, I slide toward escape. I watch his feet as I push my way to the end of the truck. He turns when I make noise.

I'm not going to make it out.

He runs around the truck and grabs my legs that are sticking out. His fingers dig into my ankles as he pulls me across the concrete on my face.

"Got you," he says in victory.

I kick and squirm, but he doesn't let go of my legs.

I twist onto my back, and he's forced to release one of my ankles. I take advantage and slam my heel into his already bleeding nose.

He drops the other foot in surprise and pain.

In an instant, I'm back on my feet.

And I'm running down the alley, so fast that the gravel slides under my feet.

Headlights glare from the end of the alley, making it hard to see. I sprint for the lights, praying it's Ford.

Footsteps pound behind me, and I feel fingers tangling in the back of my shirt.

"Stop. Police."

I recognize Ford's voice, and twist away from the hand holding my shirt.

Ford steps into the light, his body illuminated from behind. Robert sees the gun and skids to a stop.

"Put your hands up," Ford says evenly. "Nice and easy."

I don't stop until I'm behind the car and safe.

Robert puts his hands in the air, looks over his shoulder, down the alley.

Jacob is standing behind him.

"It's over, brother," Jacob says.

"But they'll take her away," Robert says.

Ford sucks in a breath of surprise. "Is that Jacob?" he asks me.

"You can see him?"

"Yes," Ford says in wonder.

"I can't let them take her," Robert says miserably. His eyes are wild and darting from Jacob to Ford.

"Don't even think it," Ford warns, seeing his agitation.

Robert drops his hands and suddenly makes a run for it. He cuts behind his neighbor's garage and through a back yard.

Ford barrels after him and I chase them both.

"Run, Robert," Jacob shouts after them.

But running is pointless. Within a few yards, Ford has closed the gap. He launches himself onto Robert's back and wrestles him to the ground.

He has Robert pinned to the grass, but his legs are kicking wildly.

"Stop resisting," Ford commands, cuffs in hand.

I jump onto the flailing legs, shove them hard into the ground.

Robert goes limp, finally giving up.

In a flash of metal, the cuffs are on his wrists.

Jacob watches soberly. "It will be okay. It will be okay," he says.

I don't think Robert or Ford can see him now. Even to my eyes, he's more mist than solid.

Ford sits Robert up on his rear and uses a radio to call for backup.

"They have someone underground," I say. "I think it's Bess."

Ford perks up at this news. "She's alive?"

"Yep, and mad as hell. There's a metal door under the truck in the garage. It must be an old fallout shelter or something."

"You locked her up?" Ford asks Robert.

His head is hanging low and he refuses to respond.

"Let's go get her," Ford says, pulling Robert to his feet. He leads him back to the garage.

We hear faint pounding and more shouting.

Ford looks at me in surprise. "She's really here. Where's the truck keys?" he asks Robert.

Robert looks away. "I'm not helping you," he grumbles.

Ford begins searching Robert's pockets and soon finds a set of keys. He pushes the lock button and the truck clicks.

"Here they are," he hands them to me.

I pull the truck into the alley and hurry back to the trap door.

There's a large lock on it. "Is the key to this on here?" I ask Robert. He looks at the ground.

Besides the truck key, there are three other keys on the ring. I try them all, but none of them work.

Bess is still banging on the door.

I bang back to let her know we are here. "We're coming, Bess. Hang on." I shout to the door.

The banging stops.

I take the phone from my pocket and see that I'm still on the line with Ford. I hang that call up and turn the flashlight on. I begin searching the garage. "There must be a key somewhere out here." I shine the beam around and it doesn't take long to find.

A large key hangs from a ring on a nail next to the main door. I grab the key, and Robert makes a sound of protest.

I know I have the right one.

I kneel on the cracked concrete and slide the rusty key into the old lock. It turns and clicks.

As soon as I slide the lock from the handle and turn, the door is pushed up from below.

Bess's face appears, a mixture of fear and anger on it. She looks with wide eyes from me to Ford to Robert. "She stabbed me," Bess wails and scrambles out of the hole.

"Let's get you out of there," Ford says and I help Bess climb out of the hole. Of all things, she has a puppet in her hand and blood running down her leg.

"It's dark," she says in wonder. "I thought it was afternoon."

What has she been through that she doesn't even know what time of day it is?

"You're safe now," Ford says in his most comforting voice. "It's over."

Bess steps away from the hole in the floor into the alley. She takes deep breaths of air.

"You're bleeding," I say, rushing to her aid.

"Mommy?" a tiny voice calls up.

"She stabbed me in the leg," Bess says. "She's crazy."

Ford and I exchange a look.

"Is there a child down there?" I ask Robert.

"Missy," he finally says. "Please don't hurt her. We did all this for her. She needs help."

"She's a murderer," Bess says from the alley. I notice the puppet is now on her hand, she's holding it up so it can look at us. "She deserves whatever they give her."

"She's a child. A sick, confused child."

I look into the hole and see a beautiful blonde girl with mussed up hair. She looks scared as she climbs the steps to the door. Her hands are empty.

"Missy, come on out," Robert calls to her.

She reaches the top of the stairs and pokes her head into the garage. I shine my flashlight on her frightened face.

"Mommy? Where are we?"

"I'm not your mommy. You killed your mommy," Bess says in a menacing voice.

"She killed Lynette?" Ford asks Robert. He nods miserably.

"She killed others, too," Bess says. "She told me several times."

"What about Jacob? Did you kill your daddy?" I ask the strange girl.

"Don't say anything," Robert commands.

Missy pushes her lips together and tears begin to well in her eyes.

"Jacob? He was here a few days ago," Bess says. "I don't understand."

"You saw him?" I ask.

"I did. He came a few times."

"Bess, Jacob is gone. He's a ghost."

She looks down at the puppet on her hand. "A ghost? I don't understand. You must be lying."

Her venom surprises me.

"I'm not lying."

"No, she's not. I'm sorry, Jacob is dead," Ford says.

"You killed him, too, didn't you?" she asks Missy.

Missy cowers behind me. "I-I didn't mean to. I don't know what happened," she cries.

"We'll get this all sorted out down at the precinct," Ford says. A squad car pulls up in the alley and Officer Frazier joins our little group.

"Detective Pierce," Frazier says to Ford, then looks at the rest of us. "Bess Freeman? You're alive."

"Looks like it," she says shortly.

"Put this one in the back of our car," Ford says, handing Robert over. "We'll be taking in the girl as well."

Frazier looks at Missy, his eyes wide in surprise. "The girl?"

"She may have killed Lynette Reed and it sounds like her father too."

With all the revelations coming at him, Frazier remains remarkably calm. He notices me and nods solemnly, but doesn't ask any more questions.

I walk Missy toward the squad car.

"What are they going to do to me?" she asks in a tiny innocent voice.

"I don't know," I tell her.

"They're going to lock you up for a long time," Bess shouts. "Like the animal you are."

Once again, I'm shocked at the venom.

"Let's let the courts decide," I say.

Bess holds the puppet to her ear like she's listening. I shudder. I don't like puppets and this one is very ugly, with big eyes and a crooked top hat.

She smiles slowly like she enjoys what the puppet is saying.

What happened to her down there? She doesn't seem injured but she's clearly going to need time and medical help to recover.

I turn my back on the strange scene and usher Missy into the car.

As I close the car door on Missy's terrified face, I feel a weight on my back. It takes me a moment to realize what's happening.

Bess has attacked me.

She pulls my hair with her free hand, and shoves the puppet into my face with her other.

"Mr. Puppet doesn't like you and neither do I," she hisses in my ear.

I spin, trying to get away, but Bess hangs on tight.

"Get off her," Ford shouts, jumping into the fight.

Ford and Frazier manage to pull her off me and set her back on her feet. I stare at her, panting. "Holy flip, what are you doing?"

The puppet is still on her hand. She is holding him up as if he is talking.

I have a sudden memory of another puppet long ago.

I grab the toy from her hand and smash it against the car, again and again.

Missy screams "no" from inside the car. Bess goes limp against Frazier.

Pieces of papier-mâché fly into the alley. I toss the remains of the puppet on the ground. As I look at it, a dark cloud rises from the broken pile.

Jacob appears as the darkness expands. He stares at it, reaches toward it.

The dark shadow grows, then surrounds him. It deepens in color, darker than the night. I watch, mesmerized as the mist envelopes Jacob's ghost.

"No, no," he wails. Darkness enters his mouth in long tendrils, drowning out his cries.

"You guys seeing this?" I whisper.

Ford scans the alley, looks right at Jacob being consumed by the blackness from the puppet. "I don't see anything. Is it Jacob again?"

The long tendrils reach deep inside the spirit, wrap around his head, entwine his body. He is consumed by the darkness.

And his spirit is gone.

I'm no longer tingling. Wherever his soul went, it's not here.

I kick the remains of the puppet. Nothing more comes out of it.

"I'm so sorry," Bess is moaning into Frazier's chest. "I don't know what came over me."

"Don't worry about it," I tell her. "You've been through a lot."

I understand more than she knows.

Half of the puppet's face, one eye and part of his nose, is staring at me from the gravel. I pick the pieces of it up and march to a nearby trash can. I lift the lid and toss the puppet in.

It's just a broken toy now, but I don't want to look at it.

THIRTY-EIGHT

It takes several days for them to find all of the bodies.

Once away from the influence of the puppet, Missy started talking. All told, Missy destroyed three of the "mommies" that were brought to her. Miss Melanie was the first. Robert liked Melanie and wanted her for himself. Missy grew jealous of her and stabbed her as she slept.

She stabbed them all in their sleep. Including her own father.

After a promise that Missy would be treated as a minor and there would be leniency, Robert started talking, too.

Robert hid the bodies in various wooded areas around the county.

And he liked Bess. He first contacted her on a dating app under a fake profile. The police techs found the contacts in her computer. The night she met up with him at The Lock Up was their first in-person encounter.

He wanted her. He drugged her. And he threw her into the bunker.

Over and over, he professed that he did it all for Missy. Once she killed her mother, he hid Jacob and Missy in the bunker. Then Missy stabbed Jacob and Robert realized he was in way over his head. He had to take care of her, but also keep her locked up. She couldn't live alone.

So when Jacob's ghost started appearing, they came up with the plan to kidnap women to care for her.

"And it all got out of hand." Ford finishes telling me the whole story the next day. We are sitting on my front porch, which is as far as I will let him into my house.

"And how's Bess?"

"She's good. She still feels terrible for jumping you. She honestly doesn't know what came over her."

I do, but I keep all that to myself.

"So it's all wrapped up. Good," I say, feeling unsettled still.

Ford finishes his root beer and sits the empty can on the table between us. "Why do I get the feeling you're not done with this?"

"I suppose it's done for Robert and Missy, but what about Melanie and Lynette? They're still here."

He looks at me sideways, his blue eyes crackling. "You want to help them cross, don't you?"

I give a half shrug I hope is cute. "That's what I do."

"Make the calls. If you don't mind, I'd be glad to help."

I'd like nothing more.

———

Mickey and Dad are easy to convince to join us. We all meet at the old church where Miss Melanie waits for the children that will never come.

She is standing behind the desk in the daycare room just like before.

"Hello, Miss Melanie. It's Rylan. Do you remember me?" Mickey has the camera trained on me. Ford and Dad stand behind her.

"Of course I do." She clasps her hands in front of her, looking for all the world like the teacher she is.

A thought pops into my head. "Why do you stay here? You can go anywhere you like."

"I am where I want to be. I like it here." She walks around the desk, runs her hands along the book shelf like I've seen her do before. "I learned to read in this room," she says. "It's one of my favorite memories." She turns suddenly. "Plus, the children. I love children and I thought they would come."

"You know they can't come."

"I know. But I can dream." She looks behind me, her eyes focusing on Ford. "You brought your boyfriend with you again. He is quite handsome."

My face flames with embarrassment and I hope the camera can't see it in the dim light. "He's not my... my anything," I say, glad Ford can't hear her.

"Too bad. He's a cute one." She turns back to the book shelf, the longing to open a book evident on her face.

"We caught the one that killed you."

She spins. "You caught Missy? You know about her?"

"We did. And we know about the puppet," I venture.

"That puppet made her do it. I just know it. That poor girl, I tried to help her. In the end, I lost."

"So you understand what happened to you?"

"I do now."

"And what we can do to help you cross over?"

She studies me for a long moment. "I suppose, if the children are not coming, I don't need to keep waiting."

I nod to Dad and he opens his Bible and starts praying. "My dad is going to say some prayers and a light is going to appear," I explain. "You just need to step into the light."

"It won't hurt?"

"No. It is beautiful." I look to Dad, Ford, and Mickey.

"Everyone focus on bringing forth the light." They close their eyes.

Dad prays.

I call to the other side with my mind.

And the light appears.

"I see it," Melanie whispers.

"I see it, too," I whisper back. "Just step in."

She takes a step closer to the light, then looks back at me. "Thank you," she says.

"My pleasure."

She looks at Ford. "Take care of that one," she says. Then she steps into the light and it swallows her.

The room falls dark.

"She's gone," I whisper, full of emotion. Everyone is so quiet I can hear them breathing. I swallow and turn to the camera to make my sign-off.

Mickey turns the camera off when I finish.

"One more," I say as Dad closes his Bible. "Lynette Reed needs to know what happened and find some peace."

"Amen," Dad says.

Jamie and her partner, Graham, must have been hard at work on the house since the police cleared it as a crime scene. The destruction in the kitchen is cleared, as is the furniture downstairs.

I feel the tingles that Lynette is close, but she must be upstairs.

"Let's check Missy's room," I say and climb the steps.

We find her on Missy's bed just like last time. "Lynette?" I ask gently. "Can we come in?"

She looks up, surprised. "I wondered if you'd come back."

"We came to see you."

"To tell me about Missy. I already know."

"How?"

"That couple that is tearing my house apart were talking about it. They said my daughter killed several people." Her voice is heavy with regret.

"I'm sorry, but it's true," I tell her.

She plucks at a piece of lint on her jeans. "I worried about her after what she did to me."

"You know she stabbed you?"

"Of course. I was there, wasn't I?"

"Yes, of course." I look at Mickey, Ford, and Dad. "Look, Lynette, you've been here in this house for a long time. We can help you cross to the other side."

She looks up, startled. "I can't go."

"Why not?" This is not what I expected.

"Someone has to look after Missy."

"She's been taken to a juvenile facility for her crimes. They'll take care of her, but she'll have to stay there for a long time."

"I will find her." She stands, ready to go now. "I can leave here, right?"

"I guess so. That's often how it works."

"Then I'll go to her. I'll watch over her."

"That's what Jacob's ghost tried to do. That's why all these terrible things happened."

"Jacob? He's a ghost? Maybe I can find him, too."

That's not possible, he was taken, but I don't have the heart to tell her. "Maybe," I lie.

"I'll find them. We can be a family again."

"I really don't think that's possible," I protest.

"You can't stop me. Goodbye, Rylan. Don't come looking for me again."

She fades into a mist, and then disappears.

"She's gone," I tell the group.

"She crossed already?" Dad asks.

"No. She's going to find Missy."

"She can't do that," Ford says. "Missy is locked away."

"That won't stop a ghost," I point out.

I'm aware of the camera on me. "Well, this one didn't go as planned," I say into the camera. "Sometimes ghosts do as they want."

We stand in the shadows of the old house, not sure what to do. Mickey turns the camera off and lowers it to her side.

"Now what?" she asks.

"Now we go home, I guess."

Ford leaves the room first and we all file out after him. On the front porch, my phone rings in my pocket.

"Sorry," I say, surprised to be getting a call this late at night. "I thought I turned my ringer off."

Dad and Ford go down the front steps as I answer.

"Hey Rylan," a voice says, one I never thought I'd hear again. "It's Declan."

"I see that," I reply lamely. Like I could ever forget his deep South African accent.

"I need your help."

"How can I help you, Declan?" I look to Mickey for her reaction. Her eyes grow wide. Ford turns in the moonlight, recognizing the name.

Besides Ford, Declan Rathborne is the only man I have ever loved.

"I think my mansion is haunted," Declan says.

A LETTER FROM DAWN

Dearest reader,

A huge thank you for choosing to read *The Shadow Girls*. I truly appreciate you. I hope you loved it. If you did enjoy it, and want to keep up to date with all my latest releases, just sign up at the following link. Your email address will never be shared and you can unsubscribe at any time.

www.secondskybooks.com/dawn-merriman

Writing *The Shadow Girls* was a bit different than writing book one. By the second book in a series, I get to do a little more story with the characters because the reader already knows them. This story was twisty and it took a little extra work for me to keep all the storylines intact and intertwined. What a ride! Missy was such a creepy little girl, how fun. I hope you love how it all turned out.

If you enjoyed *The Shadow Girls*, I would be very grateful if you could leave a review. Feedback from readers is so special. I'm genuinely interested in what you think, and it makes such a difference helping new readers to discover one of my books for the first time.

I love hearing from my readers and I interact on my Fan Club on Facebook at the link below. Join the club today and get behind-the-scenes info on my works, fun games, and interesting tidbits from my life.

Again, thank you for reading *The Shadow Girls.*

Happy reading and God bless,

Dawn Merriman

www.dawnmerriman.com

 facebook.com/dawnmerrimannovelist
instagram.com/dawnmerrimannovelist

ACKNOWLEDGMENTS

These stories may come from me, but they come to life through the help of "my team."

First, I'd like to thank my husband, Kevin. He has great ideas that truly inspire my stories. His unwavering support gets me through the sticky plot points.

To my beta reader team, Carlie Frech, Belinda Martin, Katie Hoffman, Jamie Miller, and Candy Wajer, you helped me a lot on *The Shadow Girls*. Thank you for taking the time to read the rough pages and offer insights.

A huge thank you to Bookouture and Second Sky Books and the wonderful team there. My editor, Jack Renninson, has been a huge help. Jack, thank you for all the insights to make *The Shadow Girls* as good as possible.

Thank you to my readers for choosing my stories to spend time with.

Most of all, thank you to God for giving me the gift to tell the stories. I hope I do them justice.

Thank you all,

Dawn Merriman

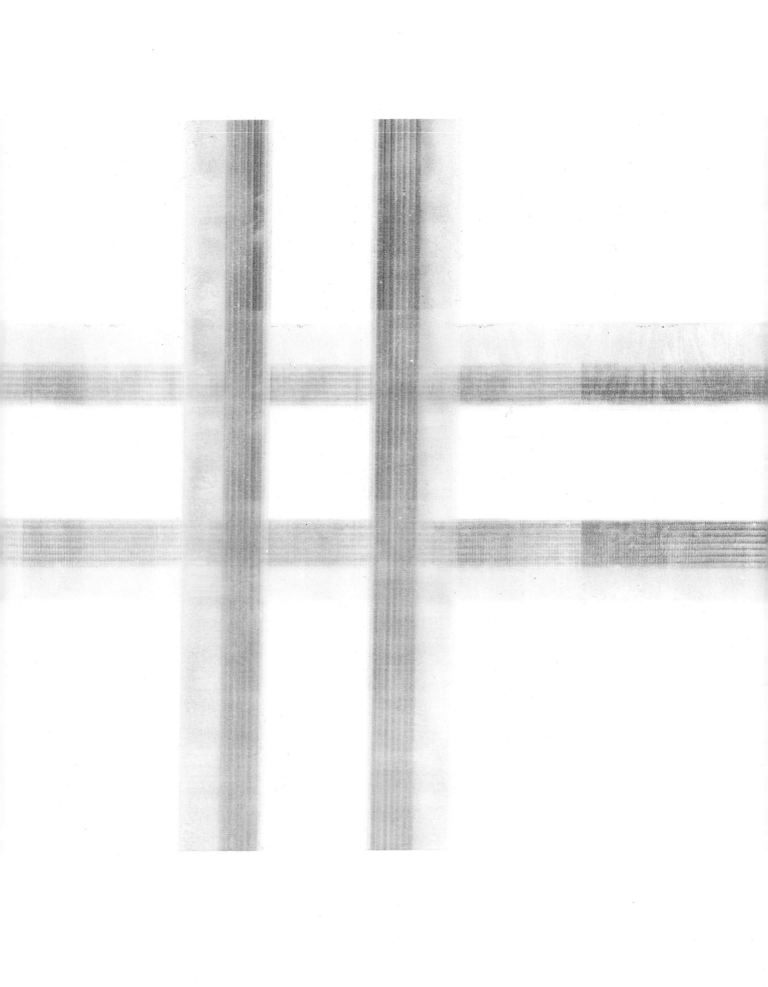